AGATHA

THE PALMER SISTERS BOOK 2

KAYT MILLER

CONTENTS

CHAPTER ONE

AGATHA

WHEN THE PHONE on my desk rings, I look down at the caller ID and see the name Miriam Smith. Strange. Why is the head of Human Resources calling me? When HR called in the past, it was usually Trent, and it was just to chat. *Wait! OMG! This is it!* I know why she's calling. I'm *finally* getting that promotion. Lord knows I've applied for enough of them. I've been here at Heart & Sole Shoes for a little over eight years. In that time, I've become a Certified Public Accountant, I've completed every class and seminar offered by HR, and I've attended every conference there is to make me the best accountant I can be. Now, all I can say is, *it's about darned time!* Shaking my shoulders out, I take in a deep breath and answer my phone, "Agatha Palmer."

"Agatha, would you please meet us in conference room three?"

"Now?" Miriam sure doesn't waste any time on small talk.

"Now."

Wow, that's strange. I guess they're anxious to get this done. "I'll be right there."

I lean down to check the time on my computer. Usually, this is the time of day I'd be heading down to the ground floor for my morning coffee. Well, not just usually—always is more like it. At precisely ten thirty every workday morning, I leave my desk and walk to the best coffee shop in the city, Java Jane's. I step in line, savoring the smells of freshly ground coffee while perusing the large, whimsical menu board on the wall above the counter. I read through each item that is painstakingly drawn with multi-colored pieces of chalk, contemplating what to get. By the time it's my turn to order, I say, "A large white chocolate mocha steamer, please." While I wait, I tell myself that *next time*, I'll order something different.

What can I say? I'm a creature of habit. My family calls me regimented, like I'm in the army or something. I disagree. I like routine—I'm used to a routine—but I can be flexible too, when need be. The truth is, they know my schedule as well as me, maybe better. They know not to call me at work at ten thirty, noon, or three fifteen. Sure, they can text me or call my cell, but they also know I keep my ringer off while I'm at work. My focus is on my job. Period. They're also aware I go to bed at eleven every night except Saturdays. Yes, it's routine, regimented, but I find comfort in that.

Standing up from my desk, I exhale to calm my nerves. I look down at my outfit. I'm wearing my one and only black pencil skirt, the one Sadie made me buy because she said I looked like a sexy librarian. Librarian, yes. Sexy, no. I paired it with a pale blue button-up blouse and my simple black pumps with the kitten heel. Looking toward my doorway, I see the jacket that matches the skirt hanging on a hook near the door. Slipping it on, I sigh in relief that I actually wore dressy business attire today. I'll look professional for this important meeting.

Before I take the elevator up two floors to the administration offices and conference room three, I stop in the restroom to double-check my appearance. I wash my hands and run damp fingers through my stick-straight hair and push my bangs away from my eyes. Fortunately, I had the good sense to pull it back into a tight bun at my nape today. Some tidying up is all it needs. My makeup, what there is of it, is neutral and professional. I look down, once again, at my skirt, blouse, and black jacket and smile. Wow, this is my lucky day. I look *good*. It's like I had a feeling something big was happening today. I button the single button on the front of my jacket and give it a tug, straightening it. "Deep breath, Agatha. You've got this."

As confidently as I can, I pull open the bathroom door and squeak in alarm as I run smack-dab into my coworker and office bestie, Camille. "Oh, shoot, Cam. I'm sorry."

Laughing it off, Camille pats my shoulder. "No, it was my fault. I was reading a text instead of watching where I was going." Stepping around me, she adds, "Want to do lunch today? I'm dying for a wrap from McGregor's."

"Sure. Well, maybe." I reach out and give her upper arm a squeeze. "I've got a meeting." I pause for dramatic effect. "Upstairs," I say excitedly.

"Oh, my God. Is it your promotion?" Camille says, hopping up and down.

"I think so. Finally." I roll my eyes but smile wide.

"You deserve it, honey. You work *so* hard."

"So do you." But the thing is, Camille hasn't been here as long as I have. She's not a CPA either. Someday I could see her moving up, just not yet.

"Nah, you deserve it." She moves further into the bathroom.

"Good luck. Be sure to stop by my cube when you get back. I want to hear *everything.*"

Since our cubicles are in the same area, that's not a problem. "Okay. Talk to you soon."

"Good luck," she sings just as the bathroom door shuts.

I walk to the elevator and press the Up button. Tugging my jacket once again, I repeat my mantra. "This is it, Agatha. Your life is about to change."

~

TWO WEEKS Later

"WAKE UP, AGATHA."

I hear a muffled voice that I just can't place.

"Aggie. Come on. Up and at 'em."

Atom? That's a funny word to use. I feel myself being gently jostled around.

"For fuck's sake, girl. Wake up!"

Wow, that one was loud and right next to my ear. I slowly open one eye to see two faces mere inches from mine.

"Wake the fuck up, woman." It's Keely. My baby sister has quite a mouth on her, that's for sure. "Where is my sister who wakes up at six in the morning, even on weekends? Huh?"

"She left the building," I mumble into the pillow.

Violet, her twin, is looking at me with furrowed brows and concern in her eyes. I open the other eye and stare for just a few more seconds. I need to think. I haven't quite figured out why they're here. Closing my eyes slowly, I do my best to remember what day it is. Friday? Is it Friday?

I push myself up a few inches, and then flop back down. I hurt. *Is it possible to get a hangover from cookie dough?*

"No, it's not. But if the number of empty wine boxes strewn about your house is any indication of your night, I'd say cookie dough is *not* the culprit."

Shit. I said that aloud?

"Aggie, get up, damn it. You stink. When was the last time you showered?" There's a pause. "Or, hell, did anything like clean, dust, do the dishes, or vacuum your house? This place looks like a tornado whipped through here."

Keely Palmer. The baby of the family. She's the smallest and the loudest. The most outspoken of the bunch, for sure. She doesn't mince words. Pushing myself up into a seated position, I look at my sisters again. "What time is it?"

"Jesus," mutters Keely. "It's after three. In case your brain turned to mush in the last two weeks, which I suspect it has, that means it's the afternoon."

"Aggs?" Violet asks tentatively.

God. All I want to do is go back to sleep, but I can't. Sighing, I respond, "What, Vi?"

"You need to get up. Take a shower. Everyone will be here in an hour."

I sit up straight, "Everyone? Will be *here*?"

"Welcome to your very own intervention, big sis. Dad, Sadie, Lainie, and Keeton are all on their way, so you'd best jump up."

Shit. "B-but...."

"We let you wallow in self-pity for as long as we could, Agatha. Now crawl out of that disgusting bed and get in the shower. Vi and I will start cleaning up."

"Fine," I grumble. As I slide off the edge of the bed, I wince. Everything really does hurt. Yeah, maybe a shower is a good idea. You know, work out the kinks.

"Jesus." I turn to see Keely stripping the sheets off my bed. "What happened to the sister who changed her sheets twice a week, every Wednesday and Sunday, like an anal-retentive clock?"

I release a loud snort. She's funny. "She died," I mumble as I lumber to the bathroom and push open the door. As I enter, I glimpse the mess and wince again. "What the hell happened in here?" Clothes are strewn all over the floor and on top of the counter. To my right, an empty pizza box lies half on its side next to the bathtub. I spy a lone slice of pizza, mostly petrified, in the box. I stare at it for a second, trying to remember how it got there and how I missed that last slice. Squeezing my eyes shut, it comes to me. I ate pizza in the bathtub one night. The thing is, I'm not sure which night.

Stripping out of my shorts and tee, I reach in to turn the water on in my shower. Testing the temperature with my fingers, I adjust it before stepping in. As I do, I moan. *It feels so good.* How long's it been? Why does it seem like it was a year ago that I was canned from my job when it was only, what, two weeks ago? The truth is, I haven't been completely sequestered. There was that time I got drunk with my sisters at Murphy's. Oh! What about the night I got drunk and met Lainie's new boyfriend, Keeton, at Keely and Lainie's place? See? I've been out.

I stand under the warm spray for a good long while. It must be too long, because I'm startled to death when a surly Keely yanks back the shower curtain.

Holding a towel, she's tapping her foot on the ground like an angry headmistress. "Really?"

"What?" Seriously. What?

"You've been standing in there for like thirty minutes. That means you've got about thirty left to get this house in order before the rest of your family gets here. You do know what Lainie's going to do if she sees your place like this?"

Lainie is the eldest sister. She took on the role of mother

when our own beloved mom died when I was eight. She was ten, too young to be a mommy. Her metamorphosis to mom happened gradually. "Yeah, okay. Let me get dressed and I'll be out." Keely's right, though. If Lainie sees my place like this and me looking like, well, like I'm depressed, she'll *literally* move in with me until I'm back to my happy-go-lucky self. No, thanks. I've lived alone for most of my adult life. I like it. Don't get me wrong; I adore my sister, more than anything, but I love her more from across town. Distance and fondness and all that crap.

After quickly dressing in leggings and an Arizona State T-shirt, I run a brush over my teeth and another one through my hair. Searching my bathroom drawers, I spot a hair tie amongst some of my makeup. Pulling my hair up into a high ponytail, I stop and stare into the mirror. I look like shit. I'm pale, which makes the dark circles under my eyes more prominent. My eyes are puffy too; they look like I've gone ten rounds with Conor McGregor. No, not really, but you can tell I've been crying off and on for the last couple of weeks. I brush my bangs down in the hopes they'll hide half my face. I'm contemplating whether I should dab on some makeup when Keely screams from the living room, "If you're not out here in ten seconds, I'm going to toss all one million of these pizza boxes out into your yard."

One million? She loves to exaggerate. I march out to the main room and spot Violet first. She's got a broom in her hand, sweeping my kitchen. I should be doing that. Movement to my right draws my attention to Keely. She's standing near the front door with a stack of cardboard boxes. Pizza boxes. There are so many, I can't see her face at all. I quickly count them. *One, two, three, four, five, six, seven, eight.* "That's not a million."

"You've got one in your bathroom and two more in your bedroom. I'd say you're getting closer to the million-pizza mark."

"On a happy note, you've got enough coupons from the pizza boxes to get one free," says a cheery Violet.

Oh, sweet Violet.

But, truth? I may never be able to eat pizza again. Or drink Franzia Sunset Blush boxed wine ever, *ever* again. Peering around the room, I count three of those boxes in various places. "I'll get the wine boxes."

We spend the next thirty minutes frantically working to clean up my house, enough time to hide the evidence of my two-week wallowing bender. My dirty clothes are hidden in my closet. The pizza and wine boxes, numerous newspapers and magazines, and the equivalent of five boxes of Kleenex have all been tossed into the trash at the side of my house. I've lit one of my favorite candles and made us a pot of coffee. Just as I flop down on the sofa, a knock sounds on the door. "I'll get it," says Violet as she walks by.

When it opens, my dad steps in first. "Hey, girls."

"Hi, Daddy," I say along with my two sisters. I stand up from the couch to meet him halfway. Kissing him on his cheek, I ask him if he wants a drink.

"Got any wine?" he asks.

"I, uh, I think I'm all out."

"No, you've got a box of something in your fridge," says Keely from the kitchen. "You want a glass too, Aggie?"

"N-no, thank you." I swallow hard. Just the thought of alcohol makes me feel queasy.

"How 'bout some cookie dough?" asks the smartass.

"No, thanks."

Just then, my front door opens. I watch as Sadie, Lainie, and Keeton, Lainie's new boyfriend, step inside. I swallow hard when I see Keeton holding several boxes. Of pizza. The sight makes me shiver.

"Ooh, pizza!" yells Keely. "Aggie's favorite."

Sister or not, just as soon as we're alone, I'm going to wring her scrawny neck.

~

MY FAMILY IS SPREAD OUT ALL over my kitchen-slash-dining-slash-living room, since no one room is large enough to contain all of us. Especially with our new addition, Keeton. The guy is mammoth. He's standing up next to my kitchen island, looking mighty uncomfortable. My house is small. Tiny, really. It's a two-bedroom bungalow but the second bedroom is so small, I'd categorize it as more of a closet or, on a good day, an office. I've got a small desk and chair in there along with an armoire for extra storage. That's about all that'll fit, to be honest. No worries; there's only me here, so it's the perfect size.

"So, Agatha," says Lainie.

Here we go.

"Yes?" I turn to face her. She's sitting in one of my two dining room chairs.

"How've you been?"

"Good."

"Have you sent out any résumés or found any jobs that sound promising?"

Wow, she cuts right to the chase. "Not yet." Pretending to be busy grabbing a slice of pizza, I bite into the ooey-gooey cheese and moan. Damn, I still love pizza.

"Have you checked out job listings?" asks Sadie.

"Not yet."

"Honey," says my dad, concern in his voice. "Will you please tell me what happened at H&S?"

Why hadn't my sisters told him? They blab everything to each other. *Everything.* I hate that about them, but the one time I need for them to blab to my dad, they don't. Traitors.

"I got fired."

"I know that, Agatha." Dad steps closer so he can sit beside me on the small sofa. Softly, he asks again. "Tell me what happened, honey."

Setting my slice down, I lean back on the sofa and look into my father's sweet eyes. I hate telling him. He doesn't deserve this. He's done his worrying. He's supposed to be enjoying life, not fretting about me, but I'm going to have to tell him.

"It'll feel good to talk it out." My dad is so wise.

"I got called into a meeting by Miriam, the human resources director. I thought I was finally getting promoted." I scoff. I'm becoming very jaded in my forced retirement.

"When I walked into the room, I realized Miriam wasn't alone. Drake Garlock, the CFO, and Trent Archer, the assistant human resources director, were at the table. My department head, Kim Reynolds, and Drake's administrative assistant, Monica, were also there."

I was surprised to see Drake in the room. The man dislikes me, but I don't know why. He had his trademark scowl on his face. I looked to Trent for some sort of reassurance but got none. In fact, he looked really nervous. He seemed to be more interested in the button on his jacket than on my promotion. When I looked at Miriam, she had no expression on her face whatsoever. I've always gotten along with Miriam. No, we didn't socialize or anything, but whenever I had a performance review, she was always pleasant. Even the times she had to tell me I was passed up for a promotion, she was nice. So, there I stood, waiting.

I looked at Dad. "Miriam asked me to sit down. So, I did." I lean forward on the sofa. "When I looked up, they all had angry expressions on their faces. Really angry. Especially Drake. He spoke first saying, 'Tell us why you did it.' I had no idea what he was talking about."

"Did you ask him what he meant?" asks Dad, moving to the edge of his seat, literally.

"I did, but he just laughed, or scoffed, I guess, is a better word. Then Miriam snapped, 'We know you took the money.' When I asked, 'What money?' Trent piped up, 'You know what money.'"

I feel a tear slide down my cheek and quickly wipe it away. I don't like thinking about this, and especially about Trent and the look of disgust on his face. I thought Trent and I... well, I thought he and I were going to be something. But not anymore.

"Keep going, Aggie. We didn't get to hear any of this either. You only told us the abridged version at Murphy's," says Lainie.

I'd met my sisters at Murphy's the day I was fired and told them some of this, but not all of it. I couldn't do it then. Hell, it's hard now—two weeks later.

"Well, there were some other things said. I'm not sure I remember the words exactly but, essentially, they said I'd embezzled over one hundred thousand dollars over a four-year period."

"A hundred thousand dollars?" chokes my father.

"Yeah. That's what they claimed."

"Did they tell you how you did it?" Keeton has moved closer to the conversation. I'm sure he knew the basic story from Lainie.

"No. They just said that I took the money, that they knew I took the money, and that they wanted me to sign a nondisclosure agreement and leave the premises immediately. If I did, they wouldn't press charges."

"Now, that's the part that gets me," says Sadie. "That's a shit-ton of money. Why wouldn't they have you arrested?"

"Gee, thanks, Sadie," I reply glumly.

"No, I just mean—"

"If it's a publicly traded company, they'd want to keep it on the down low," replies Keeton. "Stocks would be impacted at that news."

"It is public. The other reason would be to keep it out of the press," says Violet. "Bad for business."

"Did you try to defend yourself?" asks Keely. "Did you fight?"

"I told them I was innocent."

"What happened then?" Sadie asks, sitting on the back of my sofa. My entire family is all around me now.

I blush, thinking about what happened next. "I, uh, signed the NDA and I stood to leave...."

They all stare at me. The room is silent for a beat before Violet speaks. "Keep going, Aggs. Tell us the rest."

It just hit me, I'm not even supposed to talk about it with my family, thanks to the NDA. "You guys can't tell anyone any of this."

"Honey, of course we won't," says my dad as he pats my knee. "Keep going."

"Okay. Well, Drake told the security guys to escort me to my desk and to make sure I only took my personal belongings and to show me the door."

And they did that. I felt like I was a dead man walking through the office. Everyone stared at the three of us. I'm sure no one knew what was happening but by the tears running down my cheeks, they had to know something was amiss.

"Security guys? What security guys?" Lainie asks, surprised.

"Oh, there were two security guys there. I hadn't noticed them when I walked in and I'd never seen them before."

"Security? I think you mean *cops*." snaps Keely. She's got a thing about cops. The thing? She doesn't like them.

"No, just security, I think. I'm not sure."

"Same difference," Keely mutters.

"Keep going, honey. You're almost done," Dad says, squeezing my hand. "It's good for you to let this all out."

"They walked me to my desk. One of the guys was kind of gruff, so the other one sent him off to do something else, then he helped me pack up a box with my things and walked me to the elevator and down to the ground floor and out to the street. That was it."

I can't tell my family that I sobbed the entire eleven floors down. It's embarrassing. In my defense, I did it quietly. The security guy was nice enough to carry my box for me until we got outside. He set it down on the sidewalk in front of me. Just as I was about to leave, I looked at him, for the first time, really. He was handsome, ruggedly handsome, but those thoughts were for another time, another place. Anyway, I looked into his clear blue eyes and said with a shaky voice, "I—" I paused, trying to put the words together. "I did *not* take that money."

Without a word from him, I picked up my box, turned, and walked down the street. Away from a career I loved—well, liked a lot. I guess I should have been happy. I had my freedom.

After everyone leaves, I put on a clean nighty and crawl into bed. Fresh sheets feel good against my bare legs. Having a clean house feels good too. Being intervention-ized by my family wasn't as bad as I thought it was going to be. Honestly, talking it out did help, as my dad predicted. Another interesting thing that happened through the process was the realization that I, in fact, was innocent. Sure, I already knew that. What I hadn't considered was that if *I* was innocent, then someone *else* took that money. The question is, who?

CHAPTER TWO

DAMN IT. I can't sleep. No matter what I do, sleep evades me. I've tried counting sheep, putting on socks, taking off socks, getting down on the floor to do push-ups—well, *a* push-up—but none of those tricks worked. Looking at my clock for the millionth time, I groan when I see that it's almost three in the morning. "I give up." Rolling out of bed, I walk out to my living room, dragging my tired feet. Plopping my bottom onto one of my wooden dining chairs, I stare out into the darkness. "I could read." That usually puts me to sleep. "Or," I stand back up, "I could work on a puzzle." I love puzzles of all kinds: jigsaw, word search, crossword, and I especially love solving detective mysteries. So, the puzzle I decide to work on is the one at H&S.

Flipping on one of my two lamps, I scan the room in search of my phone. I haven't checked it for two weeks. I didn't have it in me to read or listen to my messages, fearing what would be there. But the time has come. I look in the usual spots, ending with my purse. Digging down into my large bag, I find it at the bottom. I tap the screen, realize it's dead, and set it onto my rapid charging station on the kitchen counter. When my phone chirps to life, I see I've got forty-seven text messages and some voicemails. The majority of the messages are from my dad and sisters. A few are from Camille. I quickly scan her texts.

The first is from the day of... *the incident.*

Camille: What's going on? Why'd you leave?
Camille: Seriously, what's going on? Someone said you were escorted out of here? Call me!

Moving to the next day, I click three more messages from her.

Camille: You need to call me, Aggie. None of this makes any sense.
Camille: Where are you? I'm hearing some really fucked up stuff. Call me.
Camille: Well, shit. I'm going to call you. I need to know if you did it. Did you steal a million bucks from the company?

A million dollars? What the hell? They told me it was just over one hundred thousand.

I click on the voicemail app on my phone and tap on her first message. *"I have no idea where you are now, but you need to know the stuff they're saying around here, and I need to know it's not true. I can't believe it's true. Call me."*

Camille's second message was sent the third day after I was fired. Her voice is hushed, a whisper. *"I can't talk long. I'm hiding in the bathroom here at work. You must be laying low. I would be doing the same thing, but you need to call me. I know you. You wouldn't do this. I overheard someone say you made up some phony companies, submitted invoices to yourself from those phony companies, and then paid them. All the money went into outside bank accounts and that, apparently, you've been doing it for nearly four years. That can't be true. Right?"*

She overheard all of that? Sweet Camille. I know it's her way of helping me. I can just picture her hiding behind one of the dozen big Ficus plants they've got around the building just to get intel. I know she'd do whatever she can to help. It's what best friends do. With that said, at least now I know how they did it. They made up phony companies, sent invoices, and then paid themselves. I think I heard her say bank accounts, plural. It's crazy. I know I didn't do that. Hell, I wouldn't know the first thing about setting up a scheme like that. Sure, I pay, or I should say paid, vendors as part of my job, for materials and supplies for the manufacturing side of the company. I paid for things like leather, textiles, synthetics, rubber, cardboard boxes, and foam. And since Heart & Sole Shoes is a Fortune 1000 company, we used *a lot* of those materials. We're an international company that supplies shoes to large department store chains, boutiques, huge online retailers, and more. I was responsible, and authorized, to pay out large bills in the tens of thousands of dollars. I guess I could see how a lot of money could be funneled through my office, but it didn't happen at *my* desk. How could it?

Stepping away from my charging phone, I lie down on the couch and put my head on the matching sofa pillow. Closing my eyes, I practice my yoga breathing. At least what I remember about yoga breathing. It's been a long time since I did yoga, or any real exercise, for that matter. Anyway, I do my best to relax and breathe. It will help me think. According to Camille, they say I paid myself using dummy invoices. Well, whoever did that had to have logged into the system with my username and pass-word, which leads me to believe that my suspect has a background in computers. Well, at least they know more about them than I do. Now all *I* need is someone with a computer background to do whatever they do to find out who else logged into my account. I know there are ways to track people down just by the computer they used. The problem is, I don't know anyone like that. Violet is pretty good with a computer, but not *that* good.

Rubbing my temples with my fingers, I force myself to think. Fact: I know *I* didn't pay those phony invoices. Fact: I know I didn't create any bank accounts. It's ridiculous for any of my coworkers to think I'd do that. But, for some reason, they do. "I'm so screwed." I adjust the pillow beneath my head and mutter, "Think, Aggie. You're good at this stuff. Prove why it *couldn't* be you." Yeah, I'm talking to myself. I've officially lost my mind. "Because *I* couldn't have done it from my work computer, I know it couldn't be me because..." I think back to my process at work. "I only work from my desk. I never work from home. It's a rule. If I had to work late to get things done, I stayed in my office to do it." On the downside, I tend to use passwords any hacker could figure out. "That was probably a mistake."

I sat up quickly. "I've got it!" I *saved* all the invoices *I* paid. All of them. I was religious about saving a copy of every invoice I paid to a folder on my desktop. "Not only that," I say, jumping up from the couch, "at the end of each week, I dragged those saved invoices onto an external device." In my case, it was onto thumb drives. *Just in case.*

I race to my little office where I left the box of stuff I brought home from my office. Kneeling on the floor, I open the flaps of the box and see the few personal items I had on my desk. There's a picture of my mom and me. I was seven or eight, not long before she died. Setting that aside, I pull out another photo of me with all four of my sisters and my dad at my college graduation. I stare at all of us, our smiles so big. They were all really proud of me.

"Crap." My nose starts to burn like I'm about to cry as the overwhelming sense of sadness hits me. They *were* proud of me. Now they must be so disappointed.

Shaking my head, I choose to ignore my depressing thoughts. I've had two solid weeks of wallowing. Enough is enough. Reaching into the box, I find the little knickknacks I had on my desk at work, gifts from people at the office. There's a perpetual daily desk calendar that tells me all the national days of the year. For example, there's Super Hero Day, Fresh Breath Day, and National Popcorn Day. Camille gave it to me last Christmas, and I love it. It makes me laugh almost every day. Heck, Camille and I wore little capes on Superhero Day. It brought a smile to our coworkers' faces. *Good times.*

Next, I grasp something cool to the touch. It's the mod-looking name plate I've had on my desk for years. I stare down at it. The sides and back are wooden, and attached to the front is a silver plate with my name engraved on the front: *Aggie Palmer.* I set the nameplate on my dining room table with the name facing me, just like on my desk at H&S. It was a Christmas gift, or I assumed it was. One Monday before Christmas a few years ago, it appeared on my desk with a small red bow on top. I asked everyone in my department if they knew who gave it to me, but no one had a clue because no one else received one. I even asked my sisters if they'd sent it to me, since no one at H&S ever referred to me as *Aggie* at work, No, at work I've always been Agatha.

I dump out the few other items in the box and see one of my blue thumb drives. I hold it up. I ordered a whole box of them in this color. It's much cheaper to order in bulk. Blue was my mom's favorite color, and now it's mine.

I turn it over in my hand and see writing. I always write

dates on each thumb drive with an ultra-fine-point black Sharpie. This one is written in something thicker, and it's not my handwriting. "It's definitely one of mine though." I roll it around in my palm, thinking. I'm tempted to plug it into my computer to see what's on it but I'm hesitant. What if it's got some kind of virus on it or something? I'm not the techiest person in the world. I can use spreadsheet applications like Excel but knowing how the inner workings of a computer function? Not in a million years.

Stepping over to my small round dining table, I place the thumb drive next to the nameplate. "Time to get organized." I walk down my short hallway to my office-slash-closet to gather up a few things. I pull out materials like my laptop, a yellow legal pad, a pencil, a blue highlighter, and a pen from my desk drawer. I find a brand-new set of index cards in there as well. Post-its and Scotch tape, for what, I'm not sure, but better to be prepared than not. I also dig out the employee phone list I printed off last year. Granted, there have been new people hired and a few have left since that time, but if this thing had been going on for as long as they said, the person responsible would be on that list. Placing everything I've collected on the dining room table, I sit down. "So, the first question is"—I begin to write as I speak—"who stole from Heart & Sole Shoes? How much did they steal? And thirdly, how and why did they frame me?"

I tap my pen on the pad like a drummer beats his snare. I'm not sure it's helping. I close my eyes to clear out the fuzz from my brain and sigh. It just doesn't make any sense. Why me? I don't have any enemies there. At least none that I know of. I was always nice to people. I kept to myself most of the time, and those I did interact with on a daily or weekly basis were my seven other colleagues in the accounting department. While we did work together, we all worked on different things at H&S.

For example, I am, or was, one of three staff accountants responsible for paying customer invoices. My work was on the manufacturing side. Camille is a financial reporting accountant. She takes care of other things like external financial reporting and the tax side for the sales department.

Laying my head back on my chair, I peer up at the ceiling, I see a cobweb that we missed when we cleaned up the place. Spiders in Northern Arizona are those of nightmares. We get everything from tarantulas to black widows and brown recluses. Heck, even common house spiders here look like a brown recluse. A shiver runs down my back as I do my best to concentrate on my blank page.

"Where do I start?" If this were one of my favorite mystery books, the crime would start the entire ball rolling. The next step is for the femme fatale to hire the private detective. I guess I'm playing both of those parts. While I don't consider myself the traditional femme fatale, a seductress in trouble, I do accept the fact that I am, indeed, a woman in a pickle.

Sighing, I stare at the phone list. I know there are people I can rule out right away. I look at Camille's name, then Trent's. They're my only friends at the company—or at least they used to be my only friends there. I assume Trent is no longer on that short list. But Camille? I haven't talked to her since that day, but her messages assure me *she's* got my back.

Picking up my pen, I make a note to ask Violet about the thumb drive. She's the tech nerd sister. After that, I sit, staring at what I've got in front of me. "A whole lot of nothin'," I mutter. The only good thing about this? I'm sleepy now. I stand up, turn off the light in my dining area, and make my way back to bed. With my head on the pillow and my legs covered by just a sheet, I close my eyes and slowly, slowly, drift off to sleep.

CHAPTER THREE

AGATHA

BY ELEVEN THE NEXT MORNING, I'm back at my small round dining table, staring. The only difference between now and last night? I've got a cup of coffee in my hand. How am I supposed to pull off this investigation? If I were Hercule Poirot, I'd use my little "gray cells," but I am no Hercule Poirot. While my namesake was a great mystery writer, I am not. I open my laptop and check my email. On a whim, I attempt to log in to my work email and am shocked to see I still have access. Scrolling through the emails since my firing, I see I'm still in the loop on departmental and company-wide emails. I click on the one from the CFO, Drake Garlock, with the subject Agatha Palmer.

TO: All Staff
FROM: Drake Garlock, CFO

RE: Agatha Palmer

Due to an unforeseen family emergency, Agatha Palmer will no longer work for H&S. If you have questions or concerns related to Ms. Palmer's work or departure, please contact me directly.

Thank you.

Wow, that was short and sweet. I guess I should feel relieved that they didn't announce to the entire company that I was accused of embezzlement. But, according to Camille, that point is moot; the word has already spread. I save the email to my desktop. I don't know why. It seems self-defeating to keep it, but I just do things like that sometimes. I'm a saver. Searching back through the emails, I see one from Camille: *Agatha? What happened? Why were you escorted out?* I search again and see several more messages from Camille. I sigh. Poor Camille.

When I see one from Trent dated about a week ago, I'm awash with sadness again. Trent. *I had hopes for me and Trent.* I click on it.

TO: Agatha Palmer
FROM: Trent Archer
Re:

Agatha, I don't know if you can still see this email, but I wanted to tell you how sorry I am about everything. I'm sorry I ever thought you were trustworthy, reliable, and, well, someone I could see myself with in the future. You disgust me. Trent

---

A hot tear rolls down my cheek. I'm not surprised he feels that way. I am surprised he wrote it in an email though. Was it necessary for him to do that? No. It was not. I had believed my maximum humiliation quotient was met a couple of weeks ago, but I was wrong.

When I look at my screen, I see the emails I *just* read disappearing one by one. "What the hell?" Clicking frantically, I attempt to open some of the remaining unread emails. But by the time I've clicked one email, they're all gone. All of them. Poof. "Shit," I mutter. Why would they start disappearing? How could I still access my account and *then* they get deleted? It makes no sense. Why now?

AFTER A MUCH-NEEDED nap and quart of double chocolate ice cream, I return to my work. The nap helped me clear my head and put things into perspective. And the ice cream? It's always good for what ails ya. Sitting back down, I stare at the items on the table. There's not much I can do right now. I've got no proof to my theory that the actual invoices I saved on the blue thumb drives will clear my name, because I don't have them. "Why didn't I grab those that day?" The proof of my innocence lies in a box in my old office filing cabinet. There are at least five years of saved invoices on those things. Enough to prove that there's no way I could have paid the fake ones.

I need to get them. Do I ask Camille to help? No way can I do that to her, but I've decided to text her since she's got to be worried sick. I've put off talking to people in my old life long enough.

Me: Hey Camille

In less than a minute, she responds.

Camille: OMG! Are you okay? I've tried emailing, calling, and texting for weeks.
Me: I know. Sorry. I was incommunicado.
Camille: Is it true? That you...
Me: No.
Camille: I knew it! But, why do they think you stole over a million dollars?
Me: I don't know.
My eyes burn. I quickly gather myself and reply.
Me: Will you do me a favor?
Camille: What kind of favor?
Me: I think I left something on my desk. Has my desk been taken away or anything?

What I really want to know about is my filing cabinet.

Camille: No. The last time I walked past your office, everything was still there.

Perfect.

Me: If you get a chance, I'm looking for a small framed photo of me and my mom.
Camille: Oh, no! You loved that photo. Of course. I'll go in there and look around right now. Give me a minute.
Me: It might be behind my computer. It slid back there a lot.

It feels wrong to say this, but I do it anyway.

Me: Or in the second drawer of my filing cabinet.

Camille: K. I'll check.

I wait for her to reply and smile a little bit. I was so clever just then—asking her to look for something in my office. That's the important piece of this. I need to get my other thumb drives back. They're in a small box in the back of my second filing cabinet drawer. Why didn't I think to get those the day I was fired? *Oh, I remember, I was a complete blubbering mess, that's why.* I've also got a folder of personal notes and letters from people I used to call friends. Now it appears only Camille remains. I hope when this is all said and done, I can sit down with Camille and laugh at it all. But not now.

Camille: No photo, hon. But they had a cleaning crew in there over a week ago. Maybe they took it.

A cleaning crew?

Me: Well, shoot. I'll have to see if my dad has another copy. I'll be bummed if I can't get it. You sure it wasn't in my filing cabinet?

See what I did there?

Camille: Nope. Just your old files and stuff.

Good. Very good. It seems they left all of my remaining things intact. Now, how do I get my hands on those thumb drives? I can't ask Camille to take them. That'd make her an accessory. That means I have to get into the office somehow without being spotted? Oh, and past security. My attention is drawn back to my phone when another text appears.

Camille: Giiiiiiirl. I'm going to miss you at the anniversary party!

Right, the party. I forgot about the H&S 50th Anniversary celebration. How could I? I was on the planning committee, and now I'm going to miss it.

Me: Damn. I forgot. Try to have fun without me.

Camille's last text is a sad face emoji. I'm sad too. *If only I could be at that party. I could sneak up to my old office.* Since the party is down in the lobby of our building, everyone would be downstairs. I sit up too quickly and get dizzy. Ignoring that, I say aloud, "If everyone is down in the lobby, that means no one will be up in the offices."

Waking my computer, I type in the H&S web address and see the notice about the anniversary. Because of that, we planned the party for this Saturday. The entire company, reps from every branch from all over the country, will be there. The planning committee, of which I was a part, decided to transform the atrium of our building into a glamorous wonderland. At least, that was my vision for the party. The company spared no expense. With that in mind, I hired a caterer that came highly recommended, a DJ, and rented a portable lighted dance floor that I was super excited about. Trent was in charge of a multi-media presentation about us, our beloved employees past and present, that will be projected on an adjacent wall and is supposed to loop throughout the night. He called it, *The Heart and Soul of Heart & Sole Shoes*. I laugh at the memory because he was so proud of that stupid title. Sadly, I won't be able to see it. Any of it. But wait! Maybe I *could* see it.

I rub my hands over my face. "How do I get in to that party?" I certainly can't walk in the front door. "I could wear a disguise." No, that's a stupid idea. I'd get five feet into the atrium and get handcuffed by that big, handsome security guy.

Oh my. I just pictured that handcuffing scenario with the hot security man, and it gave me the sexy shivers. Shaking off the fantasy, I growl at myself, "Get your head in the game, Aggie."

So I do. I make myself comfortable on my sofa so I can meditate, aka think, aka nap. But I don't nap (this time), because the idea hits me suddenly. *It's genius.* "I could infiltrate the catering staff." There will probably be a million of them scurrying around, since they're in charge of the cocktail hour, dinner, dessert, and the bars that will be set up around the huge room. "There will be so many people, no one will notice little old me." I could access the building through the back with the caterers. Once everyone is busy, I could sneak upstairs, grab my thumb drives, and BAM—I'd be out of there before dinner is even served, no one the wiser. It's perfect. Or it will be once I work through the kinks. Fortunately for me, I've got three days to prepare. *I can do this!*

CHAPTER FOUR

AGATHA

"WHAT WAS I THINKING? I can't do this," I mumble nervously to myself as I watch the catering staff unload cart after cart filled with metal pans and equipment from their truck. I'm hiding behind a concrete post at the back entrance of the high-rise building that houses H&S headquarters. Somehow, I've got to slide into the crowd of about twenty catering staff without them noticing. I peer down at myself. At least my clothes look right. I'm wearing a white button-down shirt and black pencil skirt, the same outfit that much of the catering crew is wearing. I even found a red tie at a thrift store that looked like the ones they were wearing in the photos on their company website. My tie is a deeper red, but it'll work. It has to.

Running my hands over my hair, or wig, I should say, I fiddle with it to make sure it's secure. The blonde wig is from a Halloween costume from a few years back. All five sisters dressed up as characters from *Alice in Wonderland*. Since it was my idea, I got to be Alice, Lainie was the Red Queen, Sadie was the Mad Hatter, Violet, the Caterpillar, and Keely was, of course, the Cheshire cat. The wig was originally long and straight, but now it's shoulder-length. I cut about eight inches off the thing. It doesn't look perfect, a little uneven, but it will have to do. I added a pair of my glasses to the look, since I normally wear contacts. They're old and oversized, so that helps with my disguise.

"Hey! You! Over there!"

I hear the words, but it doesn't register where they're coming from or that they're directed at me until I look over at the catering truck and see a woman waving at me. "Are you here to work or just stand around? We need all hands on deck."

I stare at the woman, who I'd gather is only a few years older than me. "Me?" I squeak.

"Yeah, come on. We need everyone working. Chop, chop," she says, clapping her hands.

Shit. This is it. It's happening. I quickly walk toward the woman and smile weakly.

"You must be new. I'm Beth," she says, holding her hand out to me.

"Ag... I mean, Abby."

Shaking my hand, Beth smiles. "Nice to meet you, Abby. Now, get your ass to work," she says with a laugh.

She seems nice. Maybe this could end up working out for me. Lord knows I need a job.

THIRTY MINUTES later and I'm having second thoughts about a career in catering. Number one, it's backbreaking work. I've carried chafing dishes, plates, glasses, and silverware from the truck to the lobby. I must have made twenty trips back and forth. And two, my feet are killing me already. I'm regretting my shoe choice, kitten heels, but they are the only black shoes I own. It isn't lost on me that most of the crew is wearing black sneakers. Smart.

"Abby?"

I'm carrying in another tray of water glasses when someone steps in front of me. "Abby?"

"Oh, hi, Beth."

"I've been saying your name for five minutes."

"Sorry. I'm just super focused on the job, I guess." I shrug. The tray of glasses is heavy and getting heavier the longer I stand still.

Ignoring my lame excuse, Beth says, "I need you to go out and help Mark set up the main bar."

"Right. I'll just take the glasses out and then I'll find Mark."

"Mm-hmm," Beth mumbles. "Thanks."

In the lobby, I set the glasses down on one of the large round tables covered in white cloth and peer around the room. It's beautiful. It really looks like a glamorous wonderland. They pulled it off. The tall atrium space that is the lobby has been transformed with twinkling lights, flowers, and candles on each table. I chose the color scheme of plum and green that's reflected in the floral arrangements as well as in the centerpieces on each table. I feel a sense of sadness looking around the room, because it's beautiful and I helped make it that way. Only now I don't get to enjoy it.

Shaking off my blues, I get back to work. "Mark. Where are you?" I have no idea who Mark is, but if I spot the main bar, he should be nearby. As I slowly scan the room, my breath catches in my throat. Trent's here and he's talking to Beth. *Of course he's here, dummy. He was on the same committee.* "Shit," I hiss. *Act natural, Agatha.*

Acting natural has never been my strong suit. I'm a Palmer

girl, after all. We're all a little high-strung. Well, everyone except Sadie. She's fairly grounded. I run my hands over my wig to make sure it's still in place. Pushing my glasses up, I feel my face heat as I search for a place to hide. I need to relax. I'm in disguise. As long as Trent doesn't look right at me, I'll be okay. Spotting the bar, I walk quickly over in search of Mark. I don't see him, so I ask hesitantly, "Mark?"

A guy pops up from somewhere behind the bar. "Yep. That's me."

He's adorable. I could see him with Violet. He's got red hair and freckles on the apples of his cheeks. He's tall too. More than six feet, for sure. Yeah, he'd be a great fit for Vi.

"Hi." I blink. "I'm Ag... Abby."

"AgAbby? That's a funny name," he chuckles.

"Abby," I correct him.

"Abby. What can I do for you, beautiful?"

Oh, stop the presses. He's one of those. A flirt. Too bad I suck at that game. Besides that, I'm not beautiful. Of all my sisters, I'd say I rank fifth in the looks department. I'm attractive, sure, if you like the boring librarian type. "I'm supposed to help you set up."

"Beth?" he says with an arched brow.

I nod. "Yep."

Shaking his head, he mumbles, "She doesn't think I can do anything." Or something like that.

"I've no idea what I'm doing but I'm a quick study. Tell me what to do."

Mark looks up and gives me a sexy smirk, "Can you cut up some fruit for me? I need garnishes."

"Sure."

"I've got everything set up in the back on the stainless steel table. Do I need to show you how to cut fruit for drinks?"

"No. I've got it." Awesome. I can go back there and hide away. Trent won't come back there. At least I hope he doesn't.

I trot back to the catering staging area, locate the table in question, and begin cutting. I'm in my own little world and almost forget why I'm here in the first place. I use the time to work through the plan again:

As soon as dinner is well underway, I'll sneak to the back stairwell and walk the eleven stories up to my old floor. I hope the emergency stairwell doors won't be locked. They shouldn't be. Not while the party is going on.

WITH THE PARTY in full swing, I'm surprised how well my plan is working. I've been able to hide, having volunteered to help expedite the food. For those of you not in the food service biz, that means I help get the food out to the waitstaff. As the crew begins to plate dinner, I excuse myself, telling one of the others I'm supposed to help Mark at the bar. No one even questions it. I take the long corridor that runs parallel to the lobby to a set of stairs. I know my way around the building, because about a year ago, I was into my Fitbit, so I took the stairs a lot. Taking a deep breath for courage, I pull the stairwell door open and step inside.

By floor four, I want to die. Why did I ever stop exercising? My thighs are burning, I've got an ache in my side, and I can barely breathe. Stopping on the landing between floors four and five, I pant, "This is ri-ri-ridiculous." Ridiculous or not, I've got to keep going. I take the stairs once again and slowly climb. I have to stop to catch my breath every other floor. Each time, I vow to start exercising the minute I'm home free. When I finally reach the door to my old floor, I sit on the step to gather myself. Sweat is dripping down my forehead. The wig is extra hot, so I pull it off and use my sleeve to wipe off the moisture. Using the fake hair as a fan, I let the little bit of air dry my skin. Too bad I can't take off this damn skirt. My ass is sweaty too. No matter. I stand up, placing the wig back on my head. Reaching for the door I tell myself, *You can do this, Aggie.*

As quietly as possible, I pull the door open and see only darkness. There are a few overhead lights on, but I think those are for security purposes. I hold my breath, so I can listen for any noise. When I hear nothing, I step onto the carpeted floor and make my way toward my row of cubicles. It's on the furthest side of the office from where I am now, so I decide to move down a small corridor created between two rows of cubes. I scan the office, and my heart pitter-pats in my chest. I miss this place. It was my home away from home for over eight years. Even though the cubes we worked in are a drab beige color and our chairs are uncomfortable, I still liked the feeling of consistency. I could always count on my days being the same, the people being the same. God knows, numbers don't change. It's probably why accounting is such a good fit for me. I can always count on numbers. No pun intended. Ha!

When I finally get to my row, I look around again, making sure the place is empty. There are no sounds anywhere around me, so I slither into my old cubicle. Everything is still there. Well, except for my personal things. My heart twists around in my chest, and I feel my eyes burning a little. How can a job elicit this kind of feeling? It was just a job.

I scan the desk that holds my computer, then move to the filing cabinet. Quietly, I open the top drawer and see everything is still there. My manuals, folders holding blank forms, and the file with my personal cards and letters. I pull that out and set it on the desk. Next, I open the second drawer. Pulling all of the hanging folders toward me, I reach back and feel the small box that holds my thumb drives. When I lift it, I notice two things:

One, it's not heavy enough, and two, there's nothing sloshing around inside. Bringing it out, I set it on the desk and pop the lid open. "Shit," I mutter. It's empty. Who would have taken them? My shoulders slump in defeat. "Now what do I do?"

Deciding to put the box back, I pull the drawer open a bit further, preparing to set it back into the drawer... and see one. A thumb drive sitting in the back corner like a lonely girl at a school dance. "Thank God," I whisper. I reach in and wrap my fingers around it, pulling it into my tight grip.

That's when I hear it. A deep voice. A man's voice. "Miss Palmer?"

Shit, I'm so busted.

CHAPTER FIVE

Ian

"MISS PALMER?"

I've been watching the little minx since she entered the stairwell on the main level. We've got cameras in three out of four emergency stairwells. The fourth set has cameras installed. Unfortunately, due to some building electrical issues, they won't go live until next week. Staring at the security monitor in front of me, I watched the door open as a blonde woman in heels and a tight little skirt stepped through. I recognized her almost immediately in spite of the terrible wig and glasses she'd donned. I'd know those legs anywhere. "What the hell is she doing here?"

"Who?" asked my partner, Jason.

I realized I said that loud enough for him to hear, and that's not a good thing. "No one."

With a deep chuckle, Jason asks, "One of your hookups, boss?"

Jason is my subordinate. One I spend way too much time with. He's twenty-six and clueless about everything except computers. I should just say yes to get him off my back. "Yeah."

"Jesus, dude. You sure get around for an old guy. Hell, we've only been on the job for a month," he snorts.

Old guy? I'm forty-one. The prime of my life. My sex drive is more potent now than it ever was in my twenties. Hell, I had no idea how good fucking could be until my late thirties. Not until after Catherine, but that sob story'll have to wait.

"Be back later."

"Sure thing. You want me to keep keepin' on?"

Keep keepin' on? What is this, the seventies? "Yeah. Keep an eye on the party. That's your focus." If his eyes are on that, and only that, he won't get his nosey ass involved with what I'm about to do. "Back in a while. Going to walk the perimeter."

"Right on, Ian."

Jesus.

I step out of our makeshift office on the thirteenth floor and consider taking the elevator down to eleven, but that'd be too noisy. I opt for the set of stairs next to the elevator, the one without functioning cameras, and walk quietly down the two flights.

I think I know where she's going. The question is, why?

On eleven, I step out into the semidark offices of Heart & Sole Shoes. My company, Phoenix Cyber Security, has been hired to consult on the recent embezzlement. Money they're convinced Miss Palmer stole after discovering discrepancies in her customer invoices. According to the CFO, Miss Palmer created several dummy companies that billed H&S. She then paid those companies money that was funneled into accounts set up in her name.

The thing is, my gut tells me she didn't do it. Not only that, the reaction on her face when they told her about the missing money was authentic. You can't make that shit up. As a trained behavioral analyst in my previous career, I can read people. Not only was Miss Palmer shocked and surprised, the employees in the room, one in particular, were especially nervous. My eye is on that person, not pretty little Agatha Palmer. The moment out on the sidewalk, when she looked me in the eye with her own pleading gray ones, only reinforced it.

Another discordant point to that entire meeting was the fact they told her there was only over one hundred thousand missing. That was Garlock's idea. They hired us to find the money, and we've only been able to locate a small portion of it—so far. We're still searching for the rest. Drake Garlock is convinced she's got it somewhere. So, now we're holed up in an office on thirteen, spending our days watching a wall of monitors while Jason does his nerd thing attempting to find out where she, or someone else, squirreled away the rest of the money. Whoever took it knew how to hide their tracks. I only have theories right now. That's one reason we installed cameras in all of the communal spaces, the stairwells, and around the office. Whoever did it will make a mistake at some point. They always do.

Garlock gave us sixty days to find the remaining cash before he presses charges against Agatha Palmer. Yeah, that's the other thing. The reason they told her it was just over one hundred thousand? So, they could have her charged later for the additional monies. It was a dick move on Garlock's part, but it wasn't my place to argue. She signed that nondisclosure agreement, which was actually more of a confession, without reading it. I wanted to step forward and whisper in her ear, *read what you're signing*. It's another reason I decided to work to clear her name. The real embezzler would never have signed a damn thing.

Right after her firing, I did my due diligence and did a background check on Agatha.

Agatha Palmer
    Age: 29
    Height: 5'5"
    Weight: 153
    Address: 166 S. Navajo, Page, Arizona 86040
    Property Type: Own
    Payment amount: $898 / month
    Driver's License State: Arizona
    Title: Accountant
    Annual Income: $51,986.00
    Years at H&S: 8
    Marital Status: Single
    Children: None
    Criminal record: None
    Social Media: Facebook, Snapchat, Twitter

THAT CHECK INCLUDED HER FAMILY, her bank account, and I staked out her house for a few nights. I learned a lot about her. I know she has four sisters, a widowed father, and no pets. Her credit is very good; she owns her little house and a small car, and she's got only one good friend, Camille, who also works here. Agatha graduated from Arizona State University with a degree in accounting and has since earned her Certified Public Accounting degree.

I also know she likes pizza. A lot. I know she was holed up in her house for days after her termination. Instinct also told me that *if* she'd taken that money and thought she'd gotten away with it, she'd have packed up and flown off to someplace like Tahiti. But she didn't. She ordered pizza and drank too much wine. (Don't ask me how I know that. I'm not always proud of my methods.) From her behavior alone, I knew she was depressed. Experience told me she'd been set up to take the fall.

As quietly as possible, I make my way to her former cubicle. I can't think where else she'd go. I know she didn't forget anything. We went through her workspace with a fine-toothed comb. There was nothing out of the ordinary there. Just manuals, memos, and customer files. She had no evidence of the phony invoices, which wasn't surprising. When I hear a filing cabinet drawer slide open, I know my instincts are spot-on. As stealthily as I can, I step toward the opening of her old cubicle. I scan it quickly, finding her leaning into her top filing drawer cabinet. I quickly take her in, head to toe, and internally groan. The woman is sexy as hell. Her legs look amazingly curvy and long for such a petite woman. The tight skirt only accentuates her assets.

I shake my head to help me focus. She reaches in and retrieves a folder, setting it on her desk. Next, she opens the second drawer, again reaching inside. She pulls out a small plastic box, one I'd searched as well but found empty. I watch as she opens the box, peers inside, and slumps in defeat. She'd expected to find something inside? She starts to replace the box and then stops, reaching into the drawer, a small gasp exiting her mouth. She found something. Something I must have missed. As she starts to retrieve whatever it is, I speak. "Miss Palmer?"

She shrieks as she jerks her head to look at me. With a voice so nervous it quivers, she asks, "Am I under arrest?"

"No. I'm not a cop."

"You're the one who escorted me out, aren't you?"

"Yes."

"You're not a cop?"

"I used to be."

"How did you know I was here?"

I ignore the question for the time being. "Why are you here, Miss Palmer?"

"You're not going to bust me?" she asks, overlooking my question.

"No, Agatha, I'm not going to arrest you. I don't have that kind of power." I chuckle.

I think I may have surprised her by saying her name as I did, because she's silent for a moment. She must not think it's funny because she's not laughing. Hell, she's not even smiling. If I had to bet, I'd say that wetness gathering around her eyes means she's the opposite of laughing. "Please don't cry. Just give me whatever you took from the file drawer and you're free to go."

"No."

"No?" I arch my brow. That response was unexpected.

"No. I need it."

"Why? It's company property. It's stealing."

She scoffs. "It's not company property. It's mine. I paid for it." I arch a brow. She must know why, because she adds, "I didn't take that money."

When her hand moves up to the wig, I expect her to adjust it but instead, she pulls it off. Her strawberry blonde hair is smooth and pulled tightly into a knot at the base of her head. Looking down at her hand that's fisted around something small, she continues, "These are my files."

"Files? What kind of files?"

"Why should I tell you? You're just going to pull me down to the station."

"I told you, I'm not a cop."

"What are you then? A private dick?"

A cough escapes me. "A private what?"

"A private detective." She rolls her eyes and mutters, "Everyone knows what a private dick is."

"I'm not a private detective. I work for a security company."

I watch her closely as she visibly stiffens. "Again, why should I tell you anything? You were the one who dragged me out of here. You work for Drake."

I step closer to her. I'm not sure why I feel the need to comfort her, but I have the overwhelming sense that I should reassure her. "I believe what you said the day you left."

"Left? I was fired. Escorted out. I didn't just *leave*."

"I stand corrected." I smile down at her. God, she's pretty. "The day you were fired, you looked me in the eye and told me you were innocent. I believed you."

I can practically see the wheels turning in her pretty head. "You did? But not anymore?"

"I still do. Now tell me what you have in your hand."

Sighing, she leans back until her ass is on the edge of her desk. "I told you. It's just my files."

"What files?"

"*My* files. My invoices. I always saved my work. I always backed everything up in case something went missing." She rolls her eyes. "Or wrong."

"You saved *all* of your invoices? *All* of them?"

"Well, I did. Most of the thumb drives are gone. I found one at the back of the drawer."

"That's what was in the box?"

She looks surprised at the question, but she answers anyway. "Yes. Five years' worth of saved invoices. Gone. This one"—she brings her hand closer to her face—"is all that's left.

I step back from her, placing my arm on the top of the cubicle wall. "Why?"

"Why what?"

"Why did you save invoices?"

She shrugs. "I just do. Or did. When I paid a bill, I saved a copy of the invoice to my desktop folder. Every Friday afternoon, I'd drag the files onto the external thumb drive. It's just an OCD thing."

Running my hand through my short hair, I turn to face her. "Can I see what you've got?"

"Why? You can't do anything."

"I think you're wrong about that."

"Why should I believe you? I have no idea who you are or why you're trying to 'help' me." She uses her fingers to emphasize the word "help."

"Meet me tomorrow." I pull a business card out of my inside jacket pocket. I hold it out to her, and she takes it. "Away from here. I'll tell you what I know. After that, you can decide if you want to trust me or not."

She rolls her pretty eyes, but instead of speaking, she just looks at me.

"All I ask is for you to meet with me once. You can make up your mind after that."

"Where do you want to meet?"

"Your house on south Navajo Avenue."

She stands upright quickly, her eyes as round as saucers. "My house? You know where I live?"

"Yes."

"Why?" she says, too loudly.

Stepping toward her, I place my palms on her upper arms. She stiffens at my touch. "Shh, you don't want to draw attention to yourself." Sliding my palms down her arms, then up again, I do my best to ease the tension I feel in her body. "I did my homework. Yes, I know where you live. If you don't want to meet there, name the place."

"Fine. Sadie Cakes Bakery on North Navajo."

"Your sister's bakery?"

Her eyes bulge a little larger than before, "Yes. M-my sister's bakery."

"I'll meet you there. Does ten work for you?"

"Ten. Yes."

"Now, put that terrible wig back on and take the northwest set of stairs. There are no cameras working in that stairwell."

"Cameras? There were cameras?"

"Yes, but don't worry about it. I'll take care of the footage. But, get going."

"Right. Thanks, Mr. um..."

"Ian. Just Ian."

"Ian. Thanks." Sliding the wig back on her head, she moves out of the office and down the dark hallway toward the stairwell.

I watch the door until I know she's gone. Quickly, I step toward her filing cabinet to search her drawers one more time. I'm going to kick my own ass for missing that thumb drive. As I exit her office, I pick up the folder she left on the desk and head back up to thirteen.

CHAPTER SIX

AGATHA

I HIGHTAIL it down eleven flights of stairs so fast I nearly fall off my heels a couple of times. I'm not sure why. I know that man, Ian, isn't following me. The question is, *why* isn't he following me? He seems to be playing some kind of game with me. Either that or he was honest up there. But I can't think about what happened upstairs right now. No, right now, I need to get the hell out of here before someone else sees me.

On the main level, I stop at the exit door, place my ear against it, and listen for voices or footsteps. When I hear nothing, I relax enough to catch my breath and use the sleeve of my blouse to wipe the sweat from my brow. I straighten my wig again and push the door open. The hallway is clear, so I quickly walk to the catering area. People are still busy working. I see they're plating up dessert now. I move around the perimeter of the space toward the back door.

I'm about to be free and clear when I hear, "Abby?"

Shit. I slowly turn to see Beth approaching.

"Oh, hey," I say, doing my best to act nonchalant. From the look on her face, I'm guessing she knows I've been MIA.

"Look. I have no idea what the hell's going on with you tonight. I know you don't work for me, because I do the hiring, since it is *my* company." She raises an eyebrow. "Here." She pulls a business card out of her pocket and hands it to me. "If you ever want a job, for real, call me. I was impressed with your work." She turns away, then back. "At least the parts where you were actually working." She smirks.

I stare down at her card. "Thanks."

I've turned to go when she adds, "If you come into the office and fill out paperwork, I'll pay you for tonight."

Looking up, I see Beth wink at me. "Thanks, Beth."

"No problem. See you, *Abby*," she says my fake name with emphasis. She knows. Damn, she should be a sleuth too.

I race the two blocks to my car, slide inside, and start it up. Tearing out of my parking spot, I refuse to think about anything until I'm home. I need to work through all of this and I can't do that *and* concentrate on my driving. It's not safe.

~

"WHAT DO YOU MEAN, he wants to help you?"

I'm talking to my baby sister, Violet. I could talk to my other sisters too, but Violet is the only one who isn't going to judge me. The other three siblings tend to overreact, especially about something as stupid as what I did last night. Yes, Violet and I are very different, but she gets me.

"He said, and I quote, 'I believe what you said the day you left.'"

"Did he say why he believed you? Does he have proof that

someone else took the money? Is he going to tell Drake Gargoyle?"

I let out a surprised laugh. I have always referred to Drake Garlock as Drake Gargoyle with my sisters because a) he looks a little like a gargoyle with his big ears, slumped shoulders, and ever-present snarling expression, and b) because he's passed me over for promotions three different times, each time promoting a man with less experience and even less qualifications. Keely calls him a misogynist, but I've got no evidence of that. I just don't think he likes me.

"I don't know if he's got proof, Vi. I'm supposed to meet him at the bakery tomorrow at ten."

"In the morning?"

"Yes, of course in the morning. Sadie Cakes isn't open at night."

"You've got a key. The question wasn't completely off-base."

"True." We all have keys to Sadie's bakery—just in case. "Are you working tomorrow?"

Violet helps Sadie out from time to time. She likes decorating cakes, and Sadie gives her free rein to design and decorate whatever she wants. I think it's Violet's creative outlet. "I can be. I don't have class until later in the afternoon."

"That'd be great. I need witnesses."

"Sure thing, Aggs. I'll be there."

When I think we're about to hang up, Violet adds, "I can't believe you wore a disguise and snuck into that party." Her voice takes on an air of pride. "You've got *cojones*, sis."

"Honestly, I can't believe I did it either. Desperate times and all that."

"Next time, call me, and I'll help you. It could have been dangerous, Aggie."

Dangerous? Shoot, I hadn't even considered that. "True."

"Whoever stole all that money isn't messing around."

"True. Okay. Yeah. I'll call you."

Violet is really getting into my case. It's exciting. "Did you look at either of the thumb drives?"

"Not yet. I'm nervous about the one I found in the box."

"Don't try to open that one. I've got an old laptop we can use. If there's a virus on it, my old dinosaur of a computer can check it. No big deal if I have to recycle it afterwards."

"I'll come to the bakery early if you want to bring that laptop. We can check it out before I meet Ian."

"Ian," she sighs. "I've always liked that name. It's Irish for John."

I choose to ignore her wistful sigh. I'm not prepared to have feelings about Ian one way or the other. This is strictly business. Serious business. "Cool. Okay, I'm going to bed. Catering is exhausting work." I laugh. "Oh, did I tell you the caterer offered me a job?"

"No. Serious?"

"Serious. I may have to take her up on it. Money doesn't grow on trees."

"You could always ask Dad."

"No way." That man still works night and day for us. He's helped each of us along the way, and now it's his turn to have some fun. "If I have to work fast food, I will. Dad has done enough for me."

"He'd love to help you."

"I know." I feel the burn of tears once again. Holding them at bay, I whisper, "That's because he's the most amazing dad in the world."

"Yeah," she says simply. "Yeah."

"Love you, Vi. See you tomorrow."

"You too."

CHAPTER SEVEN

Ian

I'VE BEEN SITTING outside Sadie Cakes Bakery since eight this morning in my company car, a nondescript black Ford Taurus. The car windows are tinted just dark enough to obscure me from any passersby. I've watched as the constant in and out of foot traffic at the bakery has finally slowed to a crawl. The business seems to be thriving, especially first thing in the morning. My stomach growls. I'd sure love a Danish right about now. Checking my watch, I decide to head inside. It'll give me a chance to order some coffee and breakfast before Agatha Palmer arrives. Grabbing my laptop case, I step out of the car and onto the pavement.

The second the door opens, I smell baked goodness and smile. The place is damn cute. The walls are painted in light blue and white stripes. There are three small round tables with chairs in the front part of the store near the large plate-glass window. Black-and-white photos in ornate white frames hang on one wall, from top to bottom. I step closer to the images and recognize Agatha right away. She's age fourteen or fifteen, if I had to guess. She's got braces on her teeth, but that doesn't stop her from grinning at whoever's taking the picture. She was adorable back then, and she's beautiful now. Quickly scanning the other photos, I see Agatha in quite a few, along with other girls who look like her. There's a man in one hugging another sister. "Must be Dad," I mumble to myself. I glimpse another, much smaller photo. Leaning in, I'd bet money it's Agatha with a woman I don't recognize. Her mother? She's very pretty. I can see the resemblance. Agatha looks a lot like her.

As I'm about to step over to look at a set of shelves covered in jars and other knickknacks, I hear a quiet voice ask, "Sorry to keep you waiting. Can I help you?"

"Sure," I say, stepping up to the glass case at the front of the small shop. Peering inside, I salivate at the selection. Confession —I've got a sweet tooth a mile long. If I could, I'd eat cookies, cakes, and candy for every meal. But I can't do that. I work out almost every day of the week just to balance out my penchant for junk food. Adding more sweets to the mix would be impossible to overcome. Luckily, I skipped breakfast today, so when in Rome.... "I'd like a glazed cinnamon twist and..." I hum to myself as I look through the first glass case filled with every donut imaginable. Scooting over to the other case, I spy Danish, cupcakes, brownies, croissants, and scones. "A cherry Danish, and one of those chocolate croissants, please."

Standing to my full height, I finally look at the woman behind the counter. She's got to be one of the sisters. I know it's not Sadie, because I saw her photo on the Sadie Cakes Bakery website when I was doing my background check on Agatha. This one is tall with reddish-brown hair. "Can I also get a large coffee?"

"Sure. Is this for here or to go?" Her voice is so soft, almost a whisper.

"Here, please."

"If you'd like to have a seat, I'll bring it out to you."

"Great."

I walk to the table farthest from the door and wait. My stomach growls again when she delivers a porcelain plate decorated with tiny blue flowers, covered with all three of my sweet treats on top. Next, she brings over a ceramic mug filled with coffee. "Free refills," she says softly. "Would you like cream? Sugar?"

"No, thanks. This looks great." I pull a napkin from the dispenser and dig in, starting with the cinnamon twist. Biting into the soft, moist treat, I squeeze my eyes shut and moan way too loud.

"That good?"

I glance up and see Agatha Palmer looking delectable in some tight yoga legging thingies, an oversized Arizona State sweatshirt, sneakers, and a smirk. "Better than good."

"I'll pass that along to my sister."

"Which one?" I nod toward the sister behind the counter. "Sadie, or the one pretending to be busy over there?"

"Sadie." She pulls the chair out and sits. "That's Violet. And yes, she's my backup."

"Backup? You a cop?"

"Ha! Funny."

Standing back up, she goes to say something to Violet. I watch as her sister grabs a muffin out of the case and plates it onto a smaller version of mine. Sitting back down, Agatha tears off a small piece of muffin and pops it in her mouth. I watch her in silence. Her mouth is perfect. Her lower lip is slightly plumper than her top lip, but that's okay. I love to suck on a plump bottom lip now and then.

Shit. Why the fuck am I going there? She's a goddamn suspect. But, damn it, she's so pretty, and her skin looks so soft. I've yet to see her in much makeup, which I like a lot. Today, her hair is pulled back in a ponytail that reaches her shoulders. It's long but not too long. It's also a shiny reddish-blonde color. It looks almost as soft as her skin. I've fantasized about this woman way too much over the last few weeks. Now that I'm up close and personal with her again, I know I won't get much sleep anytime soon.

Reaching toward me, she pulls a napkin from the dispenser. I get a whiff of her scent. It's subtle and sweet too. Fuck, my dick is in trouble.

As Violet brings Agatha a cup of tea, I say, "Ready to start?"

"Sure." She shrugs. "I have no idea why we're here in the first place."

"I thought we'd share some information."

"Share information? I suppose you want me to go first." She rolls her pretty gray eyes.

"No, I'll go first."

"Great." She leans back in her chair, dainty porcelain teacup in hand. "Begin."

I chuckle because she's damn cute when she's bossy. "I don't think you did it."

Rolling her eyes again, she sets the cup down with a clink. "I already know that."

"Fine. How 'bout this? We suspect whoever did it used your computer."

She sits up straight, her eyes growing large and round. "How? How do you know that?"

"From the information we've gathered from the network, each transaction, each invoice, was paid from your terminal."

"That can't be." She scoots closer to the table. "Unless it was done after hours and they had my username and password."

"About that...."

"What?" she snaps.

"Using p-a-s-s-w-o-r-d-1-2-3 is a terrible idea."

"Well," she huffs. "My username isn't as simple."

I arch my brow, "A-g-a-t-h-a-8-9?"

"So? Lots of people use the year they were born for their usernames," she says defiantly.

"I know." I bite into the chocolate croissant and nearly come. "Fuck, your sister can bake."

"I know," she says.

"She single?" I laugh with my mouth full.

Crossing her arms over her small chest, she scowls at me. "No."

That's okay, I kind of like *this* Palmer sister. She's spunky. "Too bad." I shrug. "So, back to the point I was making. They used your computer during the day. Weekdays."

"That's just not possible, Ian."

Damn, I like it when she says my name. "Anything's possible, Agatha."

"Except for bathroom breaks and the times I stepped away to eat my lunch, I'm always at my desk and I never take time off." She stares at the table, then back up at me. "Well, I've taken a day here and a day there for personal things. Did it happen then?"

"No." I went over the dates of each transaction. They only ever occurred on the days she was working. "You were always there."

Slapping her hand on the table, she shouts, "That's impossible! How often did it happen——where they paid the dummy invoices?"

"Several times a month. Now, tell me something."

"Several times a month," she mutters absently. Looking back up at me, she answers, "Tell you what?"

"What was on that thumb drive?"

"I told you. My invoices."

"Did you look at them?"

"Not yet."

"Why not?"

"Honestly?"

"Always."

Sighing, she runs a hand over the top of her head. "I'm afraid to."

"If you didn't do anything, what's there to be afraid of? Do you have it with you?"

She looks over at her sister. They say nothing but seem to communicate anyway. Violet steps out from behind the counter and hands Agatha the blue thumb drive. Setting it on the table, I pull out my laptop and bring it to life. "I promise we're only looking at the file names."

Agatha nods and stands from her chair to come around the table and stand behind me. Plugging in the small device, I watch for the icon to appear on my computer. Double clicking, I see the contents of the thumb drive appear on my screen in list form. There are at least three hundred files here.

"What are we looking for?" she asks so close to my ear I can feel her breath on me. An involuntary shiver runs down my spine.

"Something out of the ordinary."

She leans further over my shoulder, reading through the list. "Do you know the names of the dummy companies?"

"Yes."

Turning her head slightly, she looks at me warily, but I can't think about that. All I can think about is the fact that she's about two inches away. "And what would those be?" she asks sarcastically.

"Palmer Textiles is one."

Standing up suddenly, she rubs her hands over her face. Looking at me coldly, she sputters, "You're screwing with me."

"No. I'm not."

"What were the other names? Agatha's Rubber Company? Aggie's Shoe Box Conglomerate?"

I look at her but say nothing. She's close.

"You're shitting me," she squeaks. "Like I'd be so frigging stupid to create businesses in my own freaking name!" she shouts. Growling loudly, she throws her hands in the air. "Violet!" she shouts again. "And another thing," she pants. "I know the companies that bill us. I've been at this for eight years. I'd know if a new company just popped up in my invoices. I'd have checked—researched the new company and what we purchased from them. I wouldn't have just paid it because it was there."

I hadn't noticed Violet was no longer nearby. My focus has been on Agatha. She's putting my skills to the test. I always know what the room is doing.

Moments later, Violet and Sadie run out from behind swinging doors. "What?" says Sadie, breathless.

"Listen to this," Agatha pants. "Whoever did this had the audacity to name the companies Palmer Textiles and...." She turns to me. "What are the other ones?"

"AGG Synthetics and A.P. Leather Company."

"You're shitting me," snaps Sadie.

I shake my head. There's one other company, but I'll keep that to myself for now. The ladies look like they're going to blow a gasket over those three.

"Wow, they must think you're a fucking idiot," Sadie snarls. Turning to me, she places her hands on her hips, "Who are you?"

"Ian." She leans her head forward like she wants more, so I add, "I'm helping Agatha."

"That remains to be seen," snaps Agatha.

I guess it does. "Let's look through these files and see what we've got."

"You can just do a search." She leans back over me, typing in the letters A and G. When several invoices appear with the name AGG Synthetics, I hear her gasp. Not only that, she rests her hand on my shoulder as she clicks in the file. "Oh, my God," she mumbles. "This one is for over five thousand dollars."

I reach out and click one of the other invoices. "This one is sixty-two hundred."

Without looking up she asks, "Are all the amounts under ten thousand?"

"Yes."

Standing upright, she's still got her hand on my shoulder. I like it.

"It's because I was authorized to pay up to ten thousand without Kim's approval." Kim was her supervisor in the H&S accounting department.

"I know."

Looking down at me, her face has fallen. Gone is the spirited, defiant girl I saw just a few minutes ago. "I'm screwed."

"It may look like that, but if you tell me what you know and let me ask you a few questions, maybe we can figure this out. Together."

CHAPTER EIGHT

AGATHA

I'M SO SCREWED.

"Let's do this," Ian says as he ejects my thumb drive.

"What?"

"Let's either go to your house or my hotel room and work through what we've got."

Is he joking? I look at him but remain silent and still. Hopefully, he'll get the hint.

"Hello? You there, Agatha?" he says, waving a large hand in front of my face.

Why do I like it when he says my name? I should hate it. He's essentially the enemy.

"I'm here."

"Well? Do you want to figure this out or not?"

Damn, he's bossy. "I do. Of course I do." But I've sort of lost my will to live. They used my name in each of the phony companies. What a shitty thing for the thief to do. They were out to get me from the start.

"Your place or mine?" he says with a smirk.

"Ugh. Seriously?" I say snottily, even though there's a part of me, way deep down inside, that likes his innuendo. The man is definitely sexy—for an older guy.

"Sorry," he says, looking sheepish. In a quiet voice, he tries again, "Do you want to work on this for an hour or two? I've got to get back to H&S after lunch."

"Sure. Let's go to my house." Looking at him crossly, I add, "I know you know where it is."

"I'm going with you." We both turn to see Violet removing her blue-and-white striped apron. "Three heads are better than two."

Not only that, she's my backup. "Great." I turn to Ian. "She's super smart."

"Awesome."

Interesting. If I didn't know any better, I'd say that was sarcasm.

Violet and I beat Ian back to my place. Luckily, it's clean now, but I still find myself nervously straightening up the pillows on my sofa and secretly wishing I had some lemonade and cookies. Internally groaning to myself, I flop onto the couch, laying my head on one of my newly straightened pillows. "Vi? What am I doing?"

"Nesting."

Attempting to sit up so I can glare at her, I realize I've got no core strength and have to grab onto the edge of the couch to push myself up, all the while mumbling, "I need to work out." Once I'm sitting up, I say, "Nesting? What's that supposed to mean?"

She shrugs. "Nothing."

"Vi, seriously. What did you mean?"

With a sigh, she says, "You like him."

"No, I don't."

"Yeah, you do. He's handsome."

"Handsome? He's old."

"He's *very* handsome, okay? And he's not that old," Violet says with her hands on her hips. "I'd say he's late thirties, early forties. Besides, he likes you too."

"He does not!" I say, standing abruptly. "Take that back."

Violet releases a giggle. "No."

"Vi—" I'm interrupted by a knock on the door.

Stomping toward it, I grip the knob and wrench the door open, then look up to see Ian holding his computer case along with a brown paper sack. I take a moment to give him a once-over. Violet is right. He's handsome. Tall and lean, but I can tell there are muscles beneath his dark suit jacket. It's open at the front, and his white dress shirt sits snugly over his chest and stomach—his very flat stomach. I quickly scan lower and make a mental note that most of his height, I'd say close to six foot two or three, is in his legs. When my eyes meet his blue orbs, I see smile lines at the corners. His nose is strong and straight. Not too big, mind you. His hair is thick. Cut short on the sides, it brings out the silver at his temple. The top is longer and dark. It's a good look for him. He should be in a hair ad for older guys. His face is clean shaven, which draws my eyes right to his full lips. Full lips that are smiling, revealing straight, white teeth. Uh-oh. I think I've been caught.

I hold my breath, expecting him to call me out. Instead, he lifts up the brown sack and says, "I brought lunch."

Leaning on the open door, I know I look surprised. "I suppose you know what we both like to eat." He did investigate me, after all.

"No. I brought a few things, so you can pick."

"Oh. Thank you," I say shyly. That was nice of him. "Come in."

Stepping over my threshold, he almost has to duck to get through. I've got standard doors throughout my house, but the place is tiny. Seeing him standing in my personal space, I can't help noticing he dwarfs the place. He's turning around in a circle. Looking for what? I'm not sure. When his eye stops at my breakfast bar, he walks over and sets the bag on top. "Should we work at your table? It looks like you've got it set up."

"Sure. Let me grab another chair for Violet."

"I'm okay over here," she says, sitting on one of the stools.

I know better than to argue with her. She'd be embarrassed if I made a big deal, so I leave her at that spot. Besides, it's not like it's across the room. She's only a few feet away. "I, uh," I start nervously, "have some notes started. That's all."

"Good. We can compare what we've got and go from there."

"Good." I nod. I look up at him and wait. He's doing the same to me. Clearing my throat, I say, "I'll start."

So, I do. Going down the bulleted list I've made on the legal pad, I explain various theories that have all been blown out of the water now that I know the thieves used my computer.

"Tell him about your emails," says Violet from her perch near the kitchen island.

Looking up at Ian, I say, "I'm not sure if it's relevant but I'll tell you anyway." If Violet thinks it's pertinent, then it probably is. "The other day, I checked my work email. I was surprised I was still able to access it."

"Me too," he grumbles. I watch him write something on his own pad of paper.

"I read the one that Drake wrote about why I was leaving."

"I wrote that."

"You did?" I blink at him. "Thank you for not telling everyone I was fired."

"Drake wanted everyone to know, but I talked him down."

"Jerk," mutters Violet. When Ian looks over at her, she clarifies, "Not you. Drake Gargoyle. He's a jerk."

Ian throws his head back, releasing a lovely rumbling laugh. Once he's stopped laughing, which takes a few minutes, he adds, "He looks like a gargoyle."

"We know," Vi and I say simultaneously.

"Keep going. What happened with the emails?"

"I read one from Trent." I scowl.

"Why the angry expression? What'd his say?"

"Oh, um, nothing."

"Agatha," he says in a domineering tone. One that I should hate, but I don't.

"Ian."

"Agatha. What did it say?"

"Oh, well, it was nothing big. Just something like, "Just something about how he's sorry he thought I was trustworthy and that I disgust him. Yadda, yadda, yadda."

"Whoa," whispers Violet. "Harsh."

"Harsh is right," says Ian as he reaches his palm out to place on top of my own. "Uncalled for." Squeezing my hand, he pulls it back to his side of the table. "Was that it?"

"No. After I read those two emails, they started disappearing."

"What was disappearing?" he asks, appearing to be confused.

"The emails. By the time I was able to click on one more, they were all gone."

"Have you tried to log in again?"

"No."

He jots something else down on his pad. "Let's try now."

I wake up my old laptop and find myself at the H&S email portal. Typing in my username and password (no comment), an error message appears. "It says my username and password are invalid."

Ian nods. "Hang on." He pulls a phone from his inside jacket pocket and begins typing. "Just sending a text to my partner Jason. I'm telling him about the deleted emails and the log in message."

"Sounds like a self-destruct bug or something," Violet says absently.

"Hmm." Ian lifts his phone again and begins to type. She must have said something that makes sense to him. Good thing, because it makes absolutely no sense to me. When he's done typing, he slides the phone into a pocket inside his jacket. "Let's eat while we wait for him to get back to me."

Violet stands to walk around my small kitchen island and pulls out the contents of the brown paper bag. "Subs."

"I got one turkey, one ham, and two vegetable subs. I wasn't sure if either of you were vegetarians."

I know Violet has been eating lots of rabbit food lately; she might go for the veggies. "That was thoughtful, thank you, Ian."

He looks down at me, gives me a small smile, and adds quietly, "My pleasure, Agatha."

Violet continues to pull things from the large bag, including several small bags of chips, condiments, plastic silverware, and a plastic container with what looks like pasta salad inside.

"Let me grab some plates." I move around the island, reaching up onto my tiptoes to the cupboard next to my stove. Just as my fingers are about to make contact with the plates, I feel a big, warm body behind me. Close behind me. So close, I freeze. I shouldn't like this.

"Here, let me, shorty."

Warning bells should be going off like crazy right now. But, for some reason, they aren't. Maybe it's because my sister is two feet away. It could also be that my instincts tell me he's trying to help. From assisting with the plates to unraveling the embezzlement charges. In my heart, I know he's sincere. Still, I can't let an insult go, now can I? "I'm not short," I grumble. Well, not *that* short. Wanting to argue the point, I attempt to turn but get only halfway. His body is so close to mine, most of me is touching at least half of him. Placing my palm on the middle of his chest, I note the hardness as I gently push him away.

He obliges with a smirk. "Sorry."

"N-no problem." I scurry back to my place on the other side of the island and wait for Violet to choose her sandwich.

She selects one of the veggie subs. Looking at Ian, I ask, "May I have the turkey, please?"

I watch as Ian takes the only other stool I've got. "I'm a garbage disposal. I'll eat whatever you ladies don't want."

I snort. "Yeah, right."

Looking sincerely affronted, he says, "What's that supposed to mean?"

"You're obviously in great shape," I say, gesturing at his body. "I doubt you pig out on junk food."

"I'll take that as a compliment." He leans closer to me. "But I *am* a true junk food junkie. I have to work out twice as hard to burn everything off." He taps the end of my nose. "And do you want to know my favorite food?" He doesn't wait for me to answer. "Pizza."

I know why he said that. Either he saw the stack of empty pizza boxes at the side of my house or he's been watching me. "Stalker," I mutter.

For the second time today, Ian throws his head back and laughs. It takes him longer to get himself under control this time, but when he does, he reaches out and pats my knee. "In the private dick business, we call it surveillance."

It's my turn to react. I feel my face flush to a hot fuchsia, and

I also nearly choke to death on my one and only bite of turkey sub.

Startled, Ian jumps off the stool and stands at my back, wrapping his arms around me. I swear he's about to do the Heimlich. "I'm fine. I'm fine. You just caught me off guard."

"You sure?" he asks, leaning close while gently rubbing my back.

"I'm sure." Geesh. I reach across the countertop to grab a bag of salt and vinegar chips and see Violet's face. The only word I can use to describe her expression? Smug.

CHAPTER NINE

Ian

AS THE THREE of us eat lunch in relative silence, I take the opportunity to look at her home. Small. That's the first adjective I'd use. But, beyond that, I'd call it homey and warm, like her. Even though the furniture is small, it all looks comfortable. The deep chocolate-hued sofa is overstuffed, as is the side chair. There's a matching tufted footstool sitting in front of the chair. The pair look like they were designed and manufactured in the 1970s, due to the mod-patterned upholstery. I rather like it.

On the furthest wall is a tall bookcase that extends from floor to ceiling. It's filled entirely with books. If I had my glasses on, I might have been able to see what she's got on those shelves from here. You can learn a lot about a person from the books on their shelves. My guess? I'd say she reads a variety of genres from romances to mysteries. There are some thicker, larger tomes on the bottom shelf. Those are most likely related to her career or education.

From my spot on one of two barstools, I can see down a short hallway where there are three doors. Two bedrooms and a bath. I know as much from my research on the property. The county assessor's page told me everything I needed to know about the house, from the square footage to number of bedrooms and baths, as well as when Agatha bought the place and how much she paid. I'm no real estate mogul but I'd say she did well with her purchase. The value has gone up significantly in the five years since she purchased it.

That's another tell about this whole embezzlement scheme. If she stole the money, wouldn't she have bought something with it? A bigger house? A nicer car than her 2015 Toyota Corolla? Perhaps she'd have taken a vacation with the money, but records show she hasn't taken any extended leave in the eight years since she started working at H&S. Hell, she's barely taken sick leave. In 2017, she had to have her gallbladder removed, but only missed three days of work. Other than that, she's taken a day here and a day there, just like she said earlier.

This woman intrigues me more every day. I'm not just referring to how beautiful she is or how I keep envisioning her curvy legs wrapped around my waist. No, it's more than that, more than sex. Although the notion of sex with her could sustain me, I feel like there's more to her than meets the eye. Way more. The problem is, am I going to get the chance to find out?

I hoped Jason would have gotten back to me by now. I'm waiting for a response from him about Agatha's claim that her emails were deleted as she reviewed them. I believe her. Why would she make something like that up? Nothing is impossible when we're talking about the cyberworld. With lunch out of the way, I decide to message him again.

Me: Did you get my text?
Jason: Yep.

Me: And?

Jason: I went down and got her computer. I'm going through it now.

Me: Why her computer?

Jason: I have a theory.

Me: Are you going to tell me that theory?

Jason: Indubitably, my good man. Indubitably.

Shit, this kid drives me crazy. The other day he talked like a guy from the 1970s. Now's he's some dapper dandy from the turn of the century? Half the time I want to punch him in the face, the other half I want to hug him like he's my kid and tell him to pull his head out of his ass. He's too smart for his own good. Let me rephrase that. He's too computer smart. Common sense? Not so much.

Me: Give me a hint.

Now, before I pull my hair out.

Jason: I'm running a diagnostic. It'll take about twenty minutes. You coming back in today?

Shit.

Me: Yeah. Be there within the next hour.

Jason: Cool. I should know something by then.

"Is that about my emails?" Agatha asks as she straightens her tiny kitchen. "Can you hand me your plate?" Her hand is extended toward me, awaiting my dish. The gesture and her statement are very domestic.

"It is, but he doesn't have anything for me yet. All he said was that he 'had a theory.'" I air quote him.

"A theory is better than nothing."

"True." Damn it. I think we're done here, and that sucks. I don't have any reason to stick around. And I'd like to. Maybe watch a movie, cuddle.

I stand up so fast, I startle both Palmer women. Hell, I startled myself. What the fuck am I thinking? *I want to cuddle?* I haven't cuddled in, well, ever. Catherine certainly wasn't a cuddler. She was too busy to cuddle. Or maybe I'd call her too intense or rigid to cuddle. Not to mention too apathetic toward me to cuddle. Not that *I* tried. I fall into several of those categories too. At least I used to. Maybe nearly dying on the job changed more than my career. It certainly changed Catherine's feelings about me. Hell, maybe getting stabbed by a fucking serial killer wasn't all bad. It got me out of a loveless marriage.

"Well, I'd better get going," I say, standing. Part of me is really hoping she'll try and stop me. *Ask me to stay, Agatha Palmer.*

"Oh, right. Well, thanks for stopping over." She wipes wet hands on a dishtowel that's embroidered with little ducks. "And for helping with, um, you know, everything." She steps around the counter to stand in front of me. "And thanks for lunch too." She smiles weakly.

"Yes. Thank you for lunch," adds Violet. She hasn't said more than a word or two. The woman sure is quiet. Nothing like her older sister. That's for sure.

"My pleasure, ladies." I step to her door, which takes me no more than a few steps. "I'll be in touch."

"Oh." Agatha approaches me. "Do you want my number?"

I've got it, but I think I freaked her out about the surveillance shit. "Sure. That's a good idea." I pull my phone out of my back pocket. "I'll add your number to my contacts. I gave you my card. It has my cell and email address listed on that."

Phone poised ready for her to speak, I wait for her to tell me her digits. She looks into my eyes, but she remains silent, until, "Oh." She giggles. "You're waiting for me. It's 555-645-4270."

I type in her information, wave, and I'm out the door. I'm hoping by the time I get back to Jason, he'll have an answer for me.

CHAPTER TEN

AGATHA

"WELL, THAT WAS INTERESTING."

I'd been watching Ian walk to his car through the tiny window in my front door. "What was?" I ask absently. Turning around, I look over at Violet sitting on my sofa.

"That whole. Thing." Violet's moving one hand in a circular motion, gesturing toward my kitchen.

"What whole. *Thing?*" I mimic the gesture. I know what she's referring to, but I want to hear her confirm my own thoughts.

"He's smitten."

I release a little laugh. "That's a word I haven't heard in a while. Smitten? You think?"

"I think. He couldn't keep his eyes off you, for one."

"And for another?"

"And for another, he doted on you."

Laughing harder, I say, "Doted? You're using midcentury

words. Next you're going to say he's going to ask me to go steady."

"He should. He *will*." Standing up, she brings the computer she had on her lap with her. She sets the computer on the table and walks over to me, wrapping her arms around me. "You deserve to be happy, Aggs."

"So do you, Vi."

She doesn't respond to my comment, but instead backs away. "I've got to hit the road. I've got class in a bit."

"Right. I'll call you if I hear anything from Ian."

"Do. I'm sticking with my self-destruct bug theory, but who knows?"

"Hmm."

"Oh, did you show him the other thumb drive? The one from the box?"

"Shoot. No, I forgot."

"Well, we know it didn't blow up my computer. I'm not a programmer, so I can't tell you what all that code was about, but it was definitely some sort of HTML code. Maybe his guy can look at it?"

"I'll text him about it."

Violet's face lights up. "Ooh, yeah. It gives you an excuse to text him."

I smile slyly at my baby sis. "It sure does."

I SPEND the next hour after Violet leaves straightening up my house. I dust, vacuum my rugs, and sort out my laundry. I'll have to do a laundromat run soon. I'm down to my period panties and old sweatshirts. Pulling out my legal pad, I start a To Do list. 1) get a job, 2) do laundry, 3) text Ian, 4) groceries, 5) get a job, 6) call Dad. Tapping the pen against the paper, I try to think of more. When I can't, I grab my phone. I can knock number three off the list right away.

Me: Hi Ian. This is Agatha. I forgot to show you another thumb drive I found in the box I brought home the day I was fired.

I don't have to wait more than a couple of minutes.

Ian: Hi Agatha. This is Ian. ;)

Ha ha.

Ian: What is on it? More invoices?
Me: No, a bunch of gobbledygook.
Ian: ...
Ian: That's a phrase I haven't heard in a dog's age.

I laugh out loud. See what he did there? He used an equally old phrase. Cute.

Me: Ha ha.
Ian: What do you think this gobbledygook is?
Me: My sister says it's HTML code. You know, computer coding?
Ian: I see. Do you have it with you?
Me: Yes. Sorry, I forgot about it.
Ian: No worries. Would it be okay if I stop by after work today to get it? I can have Jason take a look at it tomorrow.
Me: Sure.

Oh, my God. *He's coming back.*

Me: What time?

Ian: A little after five, give or take.

Me: Okay. Sure. I'll have it ready for you.

Ian: Before I forget. Jason's still working on your computer. I know he's on to something because he keeps muttering things like, "Well, *I'll* be..."

Me: LOL. How old is Jason?

Ian: Why?

Me: That's an even older expression than "gobbledygook."

Ian: He's in his twenties but he says things like "Far out" and "Groovy" a lot, so there is that.

Me: Right on. He's an old soul?

Ian: Ha. No. Just an idiot.

Me: Harsh.

Ian: I suppose.

Me: Okay, it's time to hit my To Do list. My laundry isn't going to do itself. I'll see you tonight?

Ian: You will. Bye, Agatha.

Me: Bye, Ian.

Wow. I reread the exchange. That felt so natural. Like we've been doing that for a long time. I'm not sure how to process it. The good thing? I have lots of time to think about it at the laundromat. *Yay me.*

CHAPTER ELEVEN

Ian

I REREAD our text exchange and smile. I can't remember the last time I enjoyed texting. That's probably because text messaging is a double-edged sword. On one hand, it's a faster, more efficient way to communicate than a phone call. On the other, it's a sure way to find out your wife's been cheating on you with your superior. See what I mean?

"Got anything?" I ask Jason as I sip my third coffee of the day. I need to switch to water or I'll be up all night.

"You know I went through this before, right? The day she was canned."

I release a low growl. I don't like that he's being so flippant about her.

"Sorry." He clears his throat.

"And?"

"I'm going in deeper, to deleted shit."

I stand, silent. Waiting.

"It looks like some shit was dumped the day before she was, uh, let go."

"What kind of shit?"

"Well, if I had to guess, it looks like remote access coding."

"Remote access? You mean someone could get into her computer from somewhere else?"

He nods. "Exactly. Remote access software gives someone access to a computer, such as a home computer or an office network computer like Agatha's here, from a remote location. It would allow anyone to work from anywhere, controlling her mouse, keyboard, everything on her computer really." Jason scoots his chair closer to me, speaking in a hushed voice, "Not only that. This means..." He pauses for emphasis. "Your girl could be innocent."

Could be? I know she's innocent. "You don't know for sure, though. Or do you? Can you tell from the coding what it did on her computer? If it was ever used or how it was used? Or more importantly, who used it?"

"That's a lot of questions, man. I may be able to figure out who else has the software on their computer, since Drake the Douche gave us free rein here after hours. But it's going to take time."

"We've got a short list of suspects. Start there."

"Right on."

I look at my watch. Three thirty. "I'm going to check in with base and get a workout in. That is, if you don't need me."

Jason scoffs. "You only distract me. But bring me some food later, would ya? If I've got to work late, I need food."

"Sure. You want junk food or healthy?"

He arches his brow at me. "You seriously asking me if I'd rather have rabbit shit over fries?"

"It wouldn't hurt you to eat better," I mutter.

When Jason says nothing more, I leave our tiny office. On

the way to the elevator, I'm approached by a small, dark-haired woman I recognize as Camille Bartlett.

"Excuse me?" she asks tentatively.

"Yes?"

"Um. Hi," she says in a flirty tone. "I'm Camille. Camille Bartlett."

I nod. I know who she is.

"I'm Agatha's best friend."

Interesting. You'd think she'd phrase that differently. I nod again. You'd think she'd say something like, "Agatha is *my* best friend."

Stepping close to me, she whispers, "I know her. She wouldn't steal any money."

"How do you know?"

She shrugs. "I just do. She's too naïve."

Naïve is a word I wouldn't use for Agatha. To me, when you say someone is naïve, I think of words like gullible or foolish. I want to hear more. "Too naïve?"

"She's not the smartest tool in the shed." She laughs. "She's dumb. I think it's why she keeps, or kept, getting passed over for promotions."

Smartest tool in the shed? Sharpest. It's sharpest. I give this woman an inner eye roll. Besides, I've seen Agatha's college transcripts; I also saw the score from her CPA exam. Agatha isn't dumb. I find this entire conversation fascinating. Either this "best friend" is trying to throw me off Agatha's scent by portraying her as too dimwitted to have committed a crime, or she's throwing her girl under the bus. I'm just not sure which. Perhaps I need to give Ms. Bartlett a closer look. In the meantime, I think I'll give Camille something to think about. "Some of the dumbest people I know are criminals. Stupidity is the number-one criterion for thieves."

"Oh." Her face blushes to a deep pink color. "I, uh, suppose that's true."

"Nice to meet you, Camille." I step around her to the stairwell. No way I want to ride down an elevator with anyone right now. Why did that entire exchange piss me off so much?

Camille Bartlett
Age: 28
Height: 5'7"
Weight: 123
Address: Whispering Sands Apartments,
300 Sandhill Road. Apt # 2, Page, Arizona 86040
Property Type: Rental
Rent amount: $400 / month
Driver's License State: Arizona
Title: Staff Accountant
Annual Income: $39,430.00
Years at H&S: 5
Marital Status: Single
Children: None
Criminal record: None
Social Media: Facebook, Twitter, Snapchat, Tinder, Match

AFTER MY WORKOUT, I order food from a little Italian restaurant I discovered my first week here. They make the best lasagna I've ever tasted. That means Jason isn't getting fries tonight. He's getting garlic bread and pasta. And so is Agatha. I can't show up to her house empty-handed. I mean... she's gotta eat. I knock on her door and wait. I listen as her feet pad across her hardwood floors, holding my breath just a little bit. The minute the door opens, I sigh. And stare. "You look nice." And she does in a pair of snug jeans and a light sweater in the same shade of gray as her eyes.

"Thanks," she responds nervously. "Come on in, Ian."

Stepping through her doorway, I hold up the bag of food. "I brought dinner."

"Again? You brought lunch. You didn't have to—"

"I wanted to. I worked out extra hard so I could eat Italian." I smile down at her.

"It smells wonderful. Did you go to Giovanni's?"

"I did."

"Yum, I love that place," she says, pulling out the foam containers. "I wish they'd quit using Styrofoam, though."

"Agreed." I pull out one of the two stools at her small break-fast bar and sit.

"What would you like to drink?" she asks, looking up at me. "I picked up a few things at the store this afternoon, so I've got beer, wine, soda, water, juice, and milk."

"Water is fine. Thanks." When she turns away from me, I take the opportunity to check her out from head to toe. Damn, she's a beautiful girl. It's the first time I've seen her in jeans, and I'm not disappointed. I get to see the shape of her legs all the way up to her hips. They're better than I imagined. I bet they'd be even more spectacular in nothing. Then there's her round little ass. I groan, and it's audible.

"You okay over there?" she giggles. "Hungry?"

"Starving." But not for Italian.

CHAPTER TWELVE

AGATHA

OH, mama. I nearly hyperventilated when I opened the door to a jean-clad, T-shirt wearing Ian Burke. Yeah, I read his business card. I now know his last name, employer (Phoenix Cyber Security), and occupation (Senior Security Analyst). But nothing compares to the knowledge that Ian Burke can fill out a pair of Levi's better than any man I've ever seen. And I know they're Levi's because I checked his ass out when he passed me at the door. To say his ass is high and tight is an understatement. And his legs? Long and muscular. Top that off with the snug Rolling Stones tee and ding, ding, ding, we've got a hot-as-sin winner.

Taking the bag from him, I step into my kitchen. I was planning on making us something to eat. I bought some chicken, rice, and vegetables just in case, but I didn't want to risk humiliation by cooking in case he was only stopping by. As I nervously unpack the food, I ask, "Would you like something to drink?"

Why does this feel like a date? At least what I remember

about dates. My stomach is full of butterflies, my heart is racing, and my palms are sweaty. I need to calm my ass down. He's here to get the thumb drive. That's it. Well, and to eat. But, *that's* it.

When he nods, I list off the selection I purchased at the store earlier. I was careful not to spend too much money on food, but I was out of almost everything.

"Water is fine. Thanks."

Handing him a bottle of water, I open the lid of the first Styrofoam container. "It looks and smells delicious. Are they both lasagna?"

Reaching into the bag, he pulls out plastic silverware and two small foam containers. "Yeah. I also got us some garlic bread and small salads." Looking up at me, he hesitates. "Is that okay? Do you like lasagna? If not, I could—"

"No, it's my favorite. I always get it." And I do. They make their own pasta, and I'm positive the mozzarella comes directly from Italy. I hand Ian real silverware. "Would you like a plate or...?"

"Nah, this is fine, thanks." He hesitates again. "Unless you want to use plates."

"Nope. Fewer dishes to wash," I say with a laugh.

"Absolutely. Dishes are my least favorite chore," Ian says, right before he takes his first bite of pasta.

"Mine is laundry." I search the bag for salad dressing. I know I'm out. At the bottom of the bag, I see two small dressing containers. *Hurray.* Looks like Italian dressing. Perfect.

Swallowing, he wipes his mouth. "Did you get it done today? Your laundry?"

"I did. It'd been piling up for weeks, so I used several machines."

"You don't have a washer and dryer here?"

"I wish." I snort. An unattractive sound, to say the least. "There are hookups in the bathroom for a stackable, but the space is already tight in there. It's easier to go to the laundromat and do it all at once anyway."

"Maybe you could use a closet. Add laundry hookups in there. I did that at my house."

"Your house? Where do you live?" Talking like this with him feels so personal, domestic. Sure, laundry isn't personal, but when he mentioned his own home, I wanted to know more.

"Phoenix."

"Makes sense." My shoulders slump a little bit. Phoenix is a long commute from here. Why that matters, I'm not sure.

"What does?"

"The name of your company is Phoenix Cyber Security."

"It is, but we've got offices all over the country. Our headquarters are actually in Nebraska."

I laugh. "Really?"

"Yep. In the middle of nowhere."

Ian smiles, and it's breathtaking. I think it may be the first time I've seen a real smile from him, which isn't surprising under the circumstances. After all, I'm accused of stealing a million bucks and he's tasked with proving it—or disproving it, hopefully. I just need to remember this isn't a date, even if he did smile like that. Dang, his teeth are straight and white, but not perfect. You can tell he never had braces, because his eye teeth are a tad crooked. Perfectly crooked.

"So, how long have you worked for them?"

He takes a bite of food. As he chews, he looks at me. It's like he's trying to decide on his answer. I stare at his throat as he chews, then swallows. He's got a nice throat. On the thick side. "I've worked for Phoenix for just over a year."

"Only a year? What'd you do before?" I pick up my bottle of water but stop midway to my mouth. "Wait! Don't tell me. Let me guess."

He nods.

"You were an FBI agent who tracked serial killers." I laugh as I sip my water, but when I look at him, he's not laughing.

"Really?"

Nodding, he admits, "Yep. For fifteen years."

I'm in awe. "No joke, Ian. If I could get a do-over, I'd do that job."

Chuckling, Ian starts to eat again. "Why the hell would you want to do that?"

"It's always fascinated me. My dream is to go on a stakeout."

"Oh, honey. Really? Stakeouts are boring as fuck."

I blush a little. "Yes, really. Solving crimes and mysteries would be the perfect job for me. My brain is analytical."

"I get it. When I joined the Bureau, I had stars in my eyes. But I'm.... Things aren't as glamorous as mystery books lead you to believe. The paperwork alone would make you quit." He laughs again but it's restrained.

"I could see that. But were you on any major cases? Anything I would have heard about?"

Ian sets down his fork and stands. I watch as he pulls his shirt up, revealing a long scar on his torso. His firm, muscular torso. But I can't focus on that. That scar.... "Oh, my God. Ian?" I race around the island to get to him. I raise my hand, nearly touching the jagged scar before I think to ask for permission and meet his gaze. He nods. I reach out and run my finger gently over the scar tissue that runs from his right side to the center of his chest. Guessing, I'd say it was eight inches long. "It was so close to your heart," I whisper.

"It was." His voice sounds uneven. "I nearly died." He clears his throat. "They said I did, for a minute or two."

Resting my palm over the scar, I feel his heart beating rapidly. Looking into his blue eyes, I say, "Who did this to you?"

"Do you remember the Chicago Slasher?"

I gasp. "The guy who stabbed his victims multiple times?"

"That's him."

"How?"

"I was a decoy. My wife and I."

I jerk my hand away from his chest like it's on fire and step back. "Your w-wife?" Holy crap. I'm flirting with a married man. And, hey! Awesome. He's flirting back.

"Ex-wife."

"Ex-wife?"

"It's a long story. I've already told you more than most people know."

"I'm sorry, Ian."

"Me too, honey. Me too." When he pulls his shirt down, I step back around the island.

"Is that why you quit the FBI?"

"It was the other way around. The FBI quit me. I was strongly encouraged to retire. Either that or I was going to be stuck at a desk somewhere."

Attempting to improve the dark mood now surrounding us, I bite into a slice of crispy garlic bread. "Mm, so good," I mumble. "Ian Burke?"

"Yeah."

"I bet you were an amazing agent."

He gives me a shy smile and a shrug.

"Oh, you're being modest. That's cute." Smiling, I take another big bite of bread. *I bet Ian's amazing at everything.*

CHAPTER THIRTEEN

Ian

WHY THE FUCK did I tell her all that? Hell, I'm not sure Jason knows half of it. Sure, he knows I used to be an agent and that I was wounded in the line of duty, but that's about it. The Bureau kept our names out of the press, thankfully. That night was one mistake after another. For one, the Slasher got away. For another, it was the end of my marriage. That night, that *one* night, was the end. All because I tried to protect my partner, who happened to be my spouse.

Shaking my head, I stand up with my empty food container. "Garbage?" I ask with a smile. No need to ruin this nice evening.

Agatha reaches out, taking the foam box from my hand and tossing it into the trash. I watch as she quickly wipes down her countertops. When she turns back to me, she's smiling. "So."

"So." I return the smile. "Do you have that flash drive?"

Her smile vanishes, but she recovers quickly. "Of course.

That's why you're here, right?" Walking out of her kitchen, she steps over to her dining table. Picking up a blue object, she holds it out to me. "It's the same color and brand of thumb drive I use, but the writing isn't mine."

Once the device is in my hands, I ask, "You said it was code of some sort?"

"Violet thinks it's HTML." She rolls her eyes. "Whatever that is."

"I'll have Jason look at it." I'm standing stock still, waiting on what, I'm not sure. Hoping. Hoping is a better word.

"So, um..." Agatha's wringing her hands nervously. "Do you have to leave now or do want to watch a movie or something?"

"I don't have to leave right away. A movie would be good." Hell, I'm as nervous as a teen boy on his first date.

"Great." She points toward her living area, specifically her bookcase. "All of my movies are over here. Do you want to pick one?"

"You don't have cable?"

She shakes her head. "Too expensive right now."

"I see." I scan her shelves, looking at the books first. Now that I'm close enough to read the spines, I can see she does, in fact, have eclectic taste. "Lots of suspense and mystery books, huh?"

"Told you. I love a good mystery."

I let my eyes roam over her romance books, old and new, mystery, suspense, true crime, and some biographies. I pull out one on Eleanor Roosevelt and open the hard-bound cover. Replacing that, I pull out a very worn copy of *On the Road* by Jack Kerouac. "You read this one?" It's one of my all-time favorites. I've read it several times over the years.

Stepping closer to me, she looks down at her book. "I never put anything on this shelf I haven't read at least once."

That doesn't surprise me. A sense of pride rolls over me at the knowledge her books are important to her.

Taking the book from my hands, she pulls off the dust jacket and points to a name written in a pretty scripted style: Rachel Montgomery. "That's my mom, Rachel. It was her book long before she met my dad. It's one of my most treasured possessions." Her voice cracks a little bit. "She'd read her favorite passages to us sometimes, but mostly it just sat next to her bed. She must have read it a million times. She used to say it gave her wanderlust until she met my father. After that, all she wanted was to be wherever he was."

There's more written in the inside front of the book. Just below Rachel's signature it reads:

For my beautiful, inquisitive Agatha on her Sweet 16. May you always enjoy life's little mysteries. I love you with all my heart, my darling girl. I will always be with you. Mom

---

Shit, I feel the sting of tears as I read it. It's not surprising Agatha's eyes are getting a little pink from emotion. Hoping she doesn't cry, I replace the paper cover and slide the book back onto the shelf. Looking down at her, I say softly, "It's my favorite book too. Your mom had great taste."

She nods, and I can see her swallow. "So, are you a car chase, explosions kind of guy or do you prefer something more classic?"

I look above her head and see *Rear Window* by Alfred Hitchcock. Reaching up, I pull it off the shelf to see if it's the old version or the new one. "I love this movie." I hold it up, showing her the image of Jimmy Stewart holding a long-lens camera and a gorgeous Grace Kelly in the background.

"Me too. Let's watch it."

I place the DVD in her hands and watch her handle several remotes until the opening credits roll across her small television screen. When she sits on her sofa, I move to her left and sit down as well. It's certainly not a big couch. It's not a love seat either, but something in between. We're close but not touching.

"Would you like something to drink? Popcorn?"

"I'm good for now, Agatha. But, thanks." I reach out and squeeze her knee, then pull back. I'm not sure why I did that, but I wish I had kept my hand there.

Agatha leans back and throws her sock-clad feet onto her coffee table. "May I?" I point to my feet.

"Of course. Mi casa es su casa."

My house is your house. I like the sound of that. I kick off my shoes, hoping my feet don't stink. When I'm sure they don't, I stretch my legs out onto the coffee table as well. Mine extend far beyond hers. If I didn't think her petite frame was cute as hell, I'd probably cringe at the freakish difference in our legs, but I do think she's cute as hell.

"You've got a hole in your sock," she says, reaching out to touch the tip of the big toe on my right foot.

When her finger touches my bare skin, I feel a shiver. Her touch is delicate, like her. "Most of my socks have holes." I chuckle. "I need a good woman to darn them for me or something."

"No," she says with a gasp. "Ian. You didn't just say that." She's blinking at me, her expression serious.

I blink, trying to recall what I just said. When I remember, I squeeze my eyes shut. "Yes, I did, but I didn't mean it like that. I'm not a Neanderthal who expects a woman to stay home and darn my socks. I just..." I run my hands through my hair. "Shit."

When I hear her laughing, I look up. She's shaking her head while cracking up. When she calms a bit, she says, "God, I hope not. That was as a pretty sexist thing to say, Ian."

"I know," I mumble. Reaching out, I touch her knee again, letting my hand linger there a little longer. "I'm not like that. I promise, Agatha."

She's stopped laughing altogether now. Looking down at my hand, then up at my face, she gives me a small smile. "Good. Glad to hear it." Seconds after that, I've got my hand back on my lap and we're both watching the film.

CHAPTER FOURTEEN

AGATHA

PULLING the blanket up closer to my face, I snuggle in to get warmer so I can get back to my dream. The one where I'm wrapped up in big, warm arms. The one where a finger runs gently over my cheek, pushing the hair out of my face. The one that felt like lips were kissing mine. Yeah, that one. I don't remember the last time I felt so safe, cared for, protected.

The loud roar of a motorcycle outside my window startles me awake. I stare at the front window attempting to gauge the time. It's still dark. I can just make out the glow of the street-lights outside my house. I blink a few times realizing I'm on my sofa. "How'd I get...?" Oh, right. I was here watching a movie. With Ian. I quickly sit up and look around my living room. There's no sign of him. "Ian?" Maybe he's in the bathroom? Standing up from the couch, I look down at myself. I'm wearing the clothes from the night before. Of course I am. Why wouldn't I be?

I step down the short hallway and see my bathroom door wide open. "He's not here." He's gone. I think back to the night before. We were watching a movie. We were talking. It was nice, relaxed. I vaguely remember falling asleep at some point. "Yay, Agatha. Way to go. Fall asleep on the hottest guy you've ever met." *I'm such a shitty date.* Wait. That wasn't a date. Sure, he brought food. The guy's got to eat. Besides, he was just doing his job; he's here for the thumb drive. "Shoot. Did I give him the thumb drive?" I look over at my dining table and see no sign of it. "I must have given it to him." Maybe I should ask him about it in a quick text? "No, Aggie. Don't be *that* girl."

Peeking at the clock on the wall, I realize it's the middle of the night. I wonder what time he left? Thinking about the evening makes me smile. Dinner was nice. Ian was nicer. Looking over at my sofa, I see my throw blanket crumpled on top. He must have covered me up before he left. I recall feeling someone touch my face, then my lips. Or was it all a dream? If it wasn't, does that mean he actually kissed me?

Yawning, I decide to go to my own bed. At my bookcase, I take Mom's book off the shelf. Holding it close to my chest, I walk to my bedroom and change into clean pajama pants. The ones with the frolicking kittens all over them. Sadie gave them to me on my last birthday. Since she's not super demonstrative, like Lainie or even Keely tend to be, these cat pajamas are her way of showing love and to make up for the fact that I've always wanted a cat but I'm allergic. No, it's not the same, but it's the thought that counts, right?

Snuggled beneath the covers, I open Mom's book. I want to read the letter I've got tucked inside. Before she died, she wrote us each a letter to be given to us on our sixteenth birthday along with one of her most prized possessions. I got her book. Lainie was given a lamp that has a cat as the base. It sat next to Mom's side of the bed for as long as I could remember. She even had it in her room when she was a girl. Sadie got Mom's recipe box. Sadie and Mom used to spend Sundays together in the kitchen making something sweet. Mom always called her Sadie-cakes, which was the inspiration behind her bakery name.

I slide the letter out of the book and think about the twins' gifts. Keely was given her music box with the dancing ballerina inside. I recall Keely playing with that for hours on end when she was little, dreaming of being a ballerina one day. Violet got Mom's locket, one she never took off. We all thought she'd been buried with it, but when Vi got that on her birthday, we were brought to tears. It was heart shaped with small flowers carved on the top half and a small diamond embedded on the bottom. The back was engraved with the words: *Violet. Always in my heart.*

"Shit," I mutter. Thinking of all of those gifts and the thought she put into them makes me so sad.

As carefully as possible, I unfold her letter. I know I should keep this in a safer place. I've made copies, but there's something about reading from the paper she actually touched that brings her closer to me. I lift the paper to my nose and inhale. Her scent is long gone but it was there for a while. I wish I could have saved that—bottled it up. I sniffle as my eyes water and my nose gets runny. "I miss you so much, Mom."

I read.

Happy Sweet 16th Birthday, my darling Aggie!

Even though I'm not there to celebrate with you on this most auspicious occasion, I wanted you to know I'm thinking about you today and always.

Being sixteen means that you're no longer a little girl. You're a young woman now. Not that you won't always be a little girl to your dad and me. But it's possible to be both. I can only imagine the young woman you've become. If I had to wager, I'd say you're smart, beautiful, and clever.

How do I know this? Because some things never change, no matter your age. I'd like to think you got those things from me but that wouldn't be true. You got as many wonderful things from your father as you did from me, but I think I'll go ahead and claim those three for myself. :) I'm sure your dad won't mind.

Aggie, it breaks my heart that I can't be there with you, but I don't want this to be a sad letter. So, let me take the opportunity to tell you all of my hopes and wishes for you, my darling.

I wish you adventure. You're my thoughtful girl, always trying to solve life's little mysteries. I hope you will always look at life with wonder, but I also hope you take a few risks along the way, even if things don't turn out the way you'd like.

I hope you make some mistakes along the way. Mistakes help us grow and learn. Mistakes make us more interesting people. Rest assured, Aggie, no matter what happens to you throughout your life—good, bad, or ugly—I promise your father and I will always, always be proud of you.

And finally, I wish you love. Not just from your dad and your sisters but love like I found with your father. It was love at first sight, but my love for him grew the longer I knew him. He was the love of my life, my person. Rob made all my dreams come true. He gave me you, after all.

While I know each of my beautiful girls are all different, I love you all the same. Be good to your father. He loves you as much as I do. Please give him a kiss for *me. Hug your sisters tight and know that I'm in all of you.*

I love you,
      Mom.

Shit, why do I torture myself? Every time I read it, I lose it. I wonder if she'd still be proud of me if she were here now. Proud of her daughter being accused of embezzling money. I also wonder if I'll ever be able to read her words and smile. Probably not, since it seems I pull this letter out whenever my life takes a nosedive.

As gently as possible, I fold the letter and place it back inside the pages of her book. My book now. Clutching it to me, I lie beneath my sheets and let the tears fall.

CHAPTER FIFTEEN

Ian

"WHOA, you look like shit, old man. You up all night with one of your lady friends?"

This is exactly what I don't need, a guy seventeen years my junior giving me shit first thing in the fucking morning. "No. Just can't sleep on those fucking hotel beds." Not to mention the fact that I didn't get into said lumpy bed until well after three in the morning. I woke up with Agatha Palmer wrapped around me like a python. Luckily, I was able to slither out from beneath her, cover her up with a blanket, and get out of her house before she woke up. I did take a moment, before I snuck out, to watch her sleep like a creeper. I couldn't help myself. She looked so fucking beautiful. Serene. I felt a sudden surge of protectiveness right then. I'm sure that's the reason I bent down, moved the hair away from her pretty face, and kissed her lips. Yeah. That's it. Protective. *Fuck.*

"Sure. Sure. I gotcha, man. So, you wanna hear how my night was?"

"Yeah. Shoot." I take a long pull from the coffee I picked up at the coffee shop on the main level, Java Jane's. Damn good coffee.

"I found no trace of that software on the desktop computers of any of our mains."

By *mains*, Jason is referring to our main suspects. "Not shocking. They could have used a laptop."

"Correctamundo. That's why I decided to look at the server and their company cloud."

"They've got a cloud?"

He nods. "Part of their software licensing agreements, I suppose. Not uncommon."

"Here." I hand him the flash drive Agatha gave me last night. "This has some kind of HTML code on it. Can you check it out after your done with the cloud search?"

"Sure thing. Add it to the pile of shit I'm already doing," Jason says, rolling his eyes.

"You want me to call up some help for you? I think Basil is available."

"Nah, I hate that douche."

"You hate Basil? No one hates Basil! He's a pussy cat."

"He's an arrogant prick," Jason mumbles.

Jason's jealous. Basil designed an app that both big-name cell platforms picked up. My guess? Basil will be gone as soon as his giant check is in the bank. In the meantime, we've got him working for Phoenix. "As you wish, princess," I mumble.

"I heard that."

"Good." Shit, we're both bitchy today. "I gotta go. Drake summoned me again."

"Sucks to be you," Jason mutters.

It does. It really, really does. "Later."

"Later, old man."

Stepping out of our tiny office, I've got enough time to do a sweep of floors eleven, twelve, and thirteen. I don't know what I'm looking for, but it doesn't matter. If something's amiss, I'll know it when I see it. Taking the stairs two at a time, I open the door to eleven and start walking the perimeter of the floor, pretending to be on my phone. The majority of people have no idea who I am. The rumor we asked Drake to set into motion was that we were here installing and testing new software. Something our company sells and hopes H&S will purchase. It's our usual cover story on embezzlement cases. It's not necessarily a lie but it makes us appear less intimidating and keep the I.T. department from nosing into our work. Besides, glorified nerds sound sort of nice compared to cybersecurity specialists.

Since I'm able to multitask, I search my messages while using my peripheral vision to see what people are doing. I spot Kim Reynolds right away and run through her background check in my head.

Kim Reynolds

    Age: 47

    Height: 5'2"

    Weight: 163

    Address: 360 Cedar Street, Page, Arizona 86040

    Property Type: Rental

    Rent amount: $2,000 / month

    Driver's License State: Colorado

    Title: Director of Accounting

    Annual Income: $75,793.00

    Years at H&S: 6

> Marital Status: Single
> Children: None
> Criminal record: None
> Social Media: Facebook, Twitter

Why is she licensed in Colorado and not Arizona? I did some checking. Her former state of residence was Colorado. So, why, in six years, hasn't she updated that information? She could be lazy as hell. I'll need to do research if she becomes a person of interest. I need to do a check of her social media sites as well. I try to do that every day or two for each of the suspects just to see if they post pictures of new purchases, stuff like that. You can learn a hell of a lot by a person's Facebook and Twitter accounts.

I pass the aisle that houses the accounting department and step through another set of doors, taking one flight up to twelve. This floor houses the human resources department, marketing, and the design team. I sweep the perimeter, making sure to look into Miriam Smith's and Trent Archer's offices. Miriam's office is empty. When I peer into Trent's, I see Miriam sitting on the corner of Trent's desk looking rather cozy. From the little interaction I've had with Miriam, she doesn't seem like the "sit on the corner of your desk to chat" kind of woman. Trent's already checked out.

I was suspicious about the fact that several of my top suspects all lived in the same apartment complex, until I noticed a large number of H&S employees rent there. It's practically the only place with affordable rentals in the area. Mystery solved.

> Trent Archer
> Age: 28

Height: 5'11"
Weight: 193
Address: Whispering Sands Apartments,
300 Sandhill Road. Apt # 11, Page, Arizona 86040
Property Type: Rental
Rent amount: $450 / month
Driver's License State: Arizona
Title: Assistant Director, Human Resources
Annual Income: $85,580.00
Years at H&S: 4
Marital Status: Single
Children: None
Criminal record: DUI in 2010
Social Media: Twitter, Snapchat, Instagram, and
TikTok.

Jesus. TikTok? How old is that guy? I guess it's one way to go.

I stay hidden behind a concrete post, obscured from Archer's office. I can't hear what they're saying, only murmurs. That is, until Miriam laughs loud enough for the floor to hear. Apparently, Mr. Archer is a funny guy.

"YOU WANTED TO SEE ME?" I don't bother knocking on Garlock's door. It's open. Besides, he's asleep at his desk. Better not startle the asshole.

"Oh," he says, startled.

See?

"Mr. Burke. You finally decided to grace me with your presence."

Ignoring his jab, I say, "I had a message you wanted to see me this morning." Like every fucking morning.

Wiping off a bit of something from his chin, he says, "Right. I wanted an update."

"Sir, there's nothing new to report." *Since yesterday.* "As soon as I've got something, I'll knock on your door."

"What do you mean, 'as soon as you've got something'? What've you been doing? How hard is it to find the money that stupid bitch stole from me?"

There's so much wrong with that statement. The only remedy is to punch the fucker in the teeth. I hate guys like this. "We've got multiple lines at work all at once, *sir*. It takes time." I hate calling this asshole *sir*. As far as I'm concerned, you earn that level of respect, and from my background on him so far, I'm not impressed enough to respect anything about him.

Drake Garlock
    Age: 55
    Height: 5'8"
    Weight: 261
    Address: 461 Rainbow Drive, Page, Arizona 86040
    Property Type: Own
    Payment amount: $3,540 / month
    Driver's License State: Arizona
    Title: Chief Financial Officer
    Annual Income: $295,542.00
    Years at H&S: 15
    Marital Status: Divorced (2x), currently
    married to Tiffany Garlock, age 28
    Children: 3 (daughters)
    Criminal record: None
    Social Media: None

"Time's-a-wastin', Ian. You've only got forty-three days left."

Forty-four, but who's counting? "Yes, sir. I'll get it done." Turning on my heel, I don't wait for more bullshit from him. There's something about that guy. Instinct tells me he's hiding something. But what? I step out of his office, shutting the door on the way out. Outside his office, people have their heads down working, but there's no sign of Drake's assistant, Monica. Taking the long way back to the office, I scan it for anything out of the ordinary.

Rounding a corner, I spy Kim Reynolds and Drake's assistant, Monica, huddled over the copy machine. "Hey, ladies," I say loudly. The two women jump apart so quickly, Kim's body hits the shelf that holds office supplies, causing it to lurch. "Sorry." I chuckle. "Didn't mean to startle you two."

Patting her chest over her heart, Monica titters as she places her hand on my forearm. "You did startle me, Ian," she says breathlessly.

"Sorry. I just met with Drake. On my way out for a coffee. Either of you ladies need one?"

"Well, aren't you a sweetheart," coos Monica. Kim remains silent. "I'm good." She turns to Kim. "You don't need any, girl-friend." Monica giggles. "You're jumpier than a virgin on her wedding night."

I stand stock-still. That was a completely inappropriate thing to say at the office, but it puts a smile on Kim's face. "Geez, Mon, you shouldn't say shit like that at work."

Monica shrugs. "Sorry. You can take the white-trash girl out of the trailer park. But... well, you get the gist."

"We sure do," I say with a chuckle.

Monica Bellamy
    Age: 33
    Height: 5'2"
    Weight: 120
    Address: 111 Date Street, Page, Arizona 86040
    Property Type: Own
    Payment amount: $966 / month
    Driver's License State: Arizona
    Title: Administrative Assistant to CFO
    Annual Income: $38,668.00
    Years at H&S: 5
    Marital Status: Married to William (age 35)
    Children: 2 (daughter, son)
    Criminal record: None
    Social Media: Facebook, Twitter, Snapchat, Instagram

"Oh, well, gotta go," Monica says, grabbing a stack of papers from the copy machine. "I'm sure Drake's asleep again. He's got a meeting with Jim from sales in five." She rolls her eyes as she click-clacks out of the copy room.

Looking down at her feet, I can't help noticing the heels she's wearing and the red soles. Expensive heels. I don't know women's designer shit but my wife—correction, my ex-wife, loved designer clothes, so I know enough to recognize quality when I see it, and those shoes are quality. Giving me a little finger wave, she adds, "See you later, big guy."

"Yep." I watch her walk away, noting the rest of her clothing. Expensive too. Designer. Nice clothes for an administrative assistant.

I turn to see Kim's back at the copy machine. She's been

quiet the last few minutes. "How are things in accounting?" Like I give a crap. I'm sure it's not up to par since Agatha left.

Turning her head only slightly, she shrugs. "Fine."

I step closer to her so no one will be able to hear our conversation.

"Just fine?"

She's not bothering to look at me now. Copying papers seems to be riveting.

"Have people been asking questions?"

She snorts. "Of course. This place is a hub of gossip."

"What've you been telling them?"

"That she quit for personal reasons."

I nod, but she can't see me since she won't look at me. "You and Monica close?"

Twirling on the spot, she says quickly, "We're work colleagues."

I give her a shrug, "Looked like you two were huddled up about something. Care to share?"

She stares into my eyes. "I thought your job was to locate the money that Agatha Palmer stole. You're a consultant. Why do you care about our office friendships?"

"You're absolutely right, Kim." I smile brightly. "I get caught up in my job. I like to know about all the players. I can't seem to help myself." I chuckle. Pointing to myself, I say proudly, "Former FBI agent."

"Former *disgraced* FBI agent," she mumbles as she turns around.

Well, well, well, someone's done her research. Interesting. "Be careful. Wikipedia isn't a reliable source, Kim, but you probably didn't know that, did you?"

"What?" She spins around to face me again. "I know how to do research. I know all about you, Ian Burke. I have my sources too. I know what you did to your poor wife." There's a little spittle flying out of her mouth.

Poor wife, my ass.

"Like I said, make sure your sources are reliable, and don't believe everything you hear."

With that, I turn and walk out the door. I can't help wondering why Kim's so hostile.

CHAPTER SIXTEEN

AGATHA

MAKING a cup of coffee in my mini Mr. Coffee pot, I stare at the dark liquid as it slowly drip, drip, drips into the four-cup carafe. Anything to keep my mind off the fact that it's been three days since Ian was here. Three *long* days. I've been doing what I can to keep busy so I don't think about him or the other night.

When the coffee's brewed, I pull down a mug and pour myself a cup. Reaching into the fridge, I realize I'm nearly out of my favorite flavored creamer. I'll need to buy more. I can't live without it in the morning. I'm pretty damn broke, though. I could just get plain creamer or resort to using milk.

A cold shiver runs through my body. "No. Not plain, and absolutely, positively no milk." I'll just buy a smaller bottle for now. Once I get a job, I'll be able to splurge on things like food and the White Mocha Latte creamer that's *almost* as good as the ones I used to get a Java Jane's. *Almost.*

I look at the clock on my stove and see it's only seven thirty. "At least I'm up early." Which means I can get a jump on the job hunt. I've updated my resume, eliminating Heart & Sole from my list of experience, which is the real reason I haven't applied for any accounting jobs yet. How am I supposed to explain the lapse in employment? According to my employment history, I'm missing eight years of my life. Maybe I should tell them I was kidnapped by aliens? Ooh, or better yet, I was lost at sea just like that Tom Hanks movie. All I need is a new best friend volleyball. I can name it Wilson just like he did. "Yeah, lost at sea," I mumble, sipping my coffee. I'm sure people would believe that. Rolling my eyes, I realize that even though H&S didn't press charges, I'm still so screwed.

On a positive note, I've made good use of my downtime. I met Camille at a coffee shop across town, away from the office, the day before yesterday. I wore my one and only disguise of blonde wig and glasses. I couldn't very well wear my catering outfit. So, I paired the wig and glasses with skinny jeans and a lightweight, tunic-like sweater. When Cam asked me about my disguise, I told her I was doing it to protect her just in case we were spotted together. "You'll get in trouble if you're seen with me," I said as I patted the top of her hand. That's no lie. I don't want her getting into trouble just because our friendship means as much to her as it does to me.

At our rendezvous, Camille filled me in on the company gossip as it relates to me. She said the big, tall guy hired to do the audit has been skulking around. (That would be Ian.)

I replied, "Oh, yeah? I think you're talking about the security guard that walked me out. What do you mean by skulking, and did you talk to him?"

"I did." She leaned in and, with a giggle, told me, "I said you were too dumb to pull something like that off."

"Camille!" I laughed along with her. "You're terrible. Did he believe you?"

She shrugged. "No idea. But I had to say something. He's got the wrong girl." She hesitated. "Right?"

"Absolutely. I'm innocent."

She looked left and right like she was making sure the coast was clear, and then asked, "Who do you think did it?"

I shrugged. "I have no idea. I can't imagine who would be capable of such a thing, let alone who would try to frame me. I thought I got along with everyone," I added, sounding sad, like Eeyore. "Do you have a suspect?"

"Well." She leaned forward again. "Trent's been acting weird lately."

"Oh, Trent," I sighed. Camille knows how I felt about him.

"I know, hon." She squeezed my hand. "I thought you two were going to end up together. But I heard from a few other people that he's been saying some really terrible things about you."

"Oh." Well, shit. I wish she hadn't told me that.

"Which is why I suspect him," she said. "I think he dost protest way too much." She nodded knowingly. "Shakespeare."

I believe it's actually "The lady doth protest too much, methinks." I wasn't about to correct her. She got the Shakespeare part right. Camille is more of a television watcher than a reader. *The Real Housewives* is her kind of thing. I don't fault her. She's fun, sweet, kind, and my best friend. Opposites attract, right?

I spent the rest of the day, after coffee with Camille, feeling sorry for myself again. I moped and ate junky food. I tried to watch a movie, but I couldn't get into it. I napped, because why not? I secretly hoped Ian would call or stop by, but no such luck.

Then yesterday, I helped Sadie out at the bakery, since one of her employees decided that working at the ass-crack of dawn every day wasn't her cup of tea. I offered to come in again today, but she said she had it covered. I'd offer to work for her on a daily basis, but that ass-crack of dawn thing isn't really for me either. I'd do it, though, if she needed me. Plus, checking my bank account yesterday made me want to call my sister back and tell her what an asset I'd be to her little company. But Sadie was clear with all of us when she opened up her shop a few years ago that she didn't want to depend on family to help her run the place. She was determined to do it on her own. Honestly? I don't get what the big deal is. What's family for? Well, correction, I do know what the deal is. It's her boyfriend, Andrew. Stuffy, fancy Andrew. He turned his nose up at the notion that his future wife would want to own and operate a bakery. According to Sadie, he's determined she'll be a home-maker after they're married. A *homemaker*? Who says that shit nowadays? Oh, right, Andrew Winchester, that's who.

So, here I sit contemplating. My bank account isn't empty yet, but after I make the next house payment, car payment, insurance payments, my cell phone bill, buy groceries, and pay my credit card, it'll be at a scary level. Rummaging through the pile of papers and items on my table, I dig out the card. "Beth Zimmer. Class Act Catering." Now that I know what the job entails, I'm sure I can do it. At least until something else pans out. Picking up my cell phone, I dial Beth Zimmer's number. It rings several times, then a canned voice message begins. I wait for the beep so I can leave my message. "Um, Beth? This is Aggie." *Shit.* "I mean Abby from the party at Heart & Sole Shoes. You said—"

I hear clicking and then, "Hello?"

"Oh, hello, yes, may I speak to Beth Zimmer?"

"You got her. You said this was Abby?"

"It's Agatha, actually."

"Ah, I see. I'm dying to ask what the hell was up with all of that the other night, but I'll wait until I've got you here to quiz you. You coming in to fill out your W-2?"

"Right, yes." Yippee! I can get paid for that night. "And to talk to you about a job."

"Great. We're in Tuba City."

"I see that." The company address lists Tuba City, Arizona, as the home base.

"Can you come in today? If you do, I've got a gig tomorrow night in Flagstaff, if you're interested."

"How much do you pay, if you don't mind me asking?"

"Not at all. It's eleven dollars per hour plus gratuity."

"Gratuity?"

"We split the tip."

"Okay. I'm about an hour and half from you." I look at the clock I calculate the time it'll take to shower, change, fill up my gas tank, and grab a fresh coffee. "I can be at your place at around ten this morning. Does that sound okay?"

"Sure thing. See you then."

I hang up the phone, jump up and down a couple of times, and squeal, "I've got a job!" A sense of relief washes over me. Relief that I'll be able to pay my bills while I figure out what's going on with the investigation and Ian.

"SO, you're going to be a caterer now?" Keely asks as she gingerly sips beer from the glass that Sadie filled to the brim.

I spent a good part of my day in Tuba City. Beth was cool; I liked her a lot. She reminded me a great deal of Sadie. No-nonsense and hardworking. Her company is small but well-established in north-central Arizona. I suppose that's why we hired her; she came highly recommended. When I told her my story, she looked a little apprehensive. I don't blame her. I assured her I was working on clearing my name. In the meantime, I had to eat. She was still willing to give me a chance, and for that, I'm extremely grateful.

When I got home, I ate some soup and took a nap. My ringing phone woke me up at around four with an invite to meet my sisters at Murphy's Pub for an evening of beer, wings, and girl talk. Yeah, I know I can't afford it, but spending time with my sibs? Priceless.

"So, you're going to be a caterer now?" Lainie asks, repeating Keely's question.

"Oh, sorry." I chuckle. "I was spacing off. So, yeah, for now I'll work banquets and parties. It's only temporary. I need money coming in, and that's not going to happen if I sit on my ass at home."

"Aggs, I'm sorry I didn't offer you the job at the bakery. If I'd known you were that worried about money...." Sadie looks sincerely torn. "I just like it—"

"I know. It's your place. I'm not financially in trouble yet. Just know that I'm happy to fill in when you need me."

Squeezing my hand, Sadie smiles. "Thanks." She takes a drink from her frosty mug, adding, "You can work when Andrew and I are on the cruise. If you don't have a real job by then, that is."

"Catering *is* a real job." Why am I defending caterers now?

"You know what I mean," she says with a scowl. "You're a CPA. You do my taxes."

"Hey, that's it!" says Lainie. "You could start doing taxes for people. I'm sure Keeton would hire you."

"Stop," I say with a chuckle. "Thank you so much, my sweet sisters, but you know I hate doing taxes."

"Right," says Lainie.

"Of course," adds Sadie.

"*Welp!* Keep it in mind if you get desperate." That one was Keely. Of course she'd say that.

I turn to Violet, who's been exceptionally quiet tonight. That's saying something, because Violet is always quiet. Well, not always. She used to be much more talkative when we were growing up. At some point, she just stopped being like that and sort of turned in on herself. When did that happen? Was it her first go-around at college? I stare at my little sister. When *did* she stop being talkative?

"Hey, Vi?"

"Yeah?" she asks, giving me a small smile.

I've been thinking about the gifts Mom gave each of us. I know Lainie keeps hers in her room. Sadie obviously has her recipe box at the shop, prominently displayed at the bakery. Keely's got her music box on the mantle above her faux fireplace, and I can't help wondering... "Where's Mom's locket? I don't see you wear it anymore."

Her smile vanishes, and she responds abruptly, "I lost it," and then stands up suddenly. "I need to, um.... I'll be back in a minute."

My sisters are chattering amongst themselves. I don't think they noticed my exchange with Violet until I look at Sadie. Her mouth is closed into a thin line. She pulls her phone out from somewhere and starts to type. When my phone dings, I know it's from her.

Sadie: I heard your question. She hasn't worn it in a few years.

Me: She said she lost it.

Sadie: Bullshit. She'd never lose that necklace.

Me: Okay. Then where is it?

Sadie: Ask Keely.

Me: *You* ask Keely.

The last thing I want to do is upset Violet with questions about her necklace. She was already put out of sorts by my simple question. I watch as Sadie types. When Keely's phone chimes, she leans down to read her phone that's sitting on the table in front of her. Keels doesn't even bother texting. "She hasn't worn it in years. It's broken. At least the chain is."

I lean forward to whisper, "She just told me she lost it."

"Nope. It's in her jewelry box. I saw it when I was looking for a pair of earrings to borrow."

"Why would she tell Aggie she lost it?" asks Lainie.

"Who knows? Chick is weird," Keely says, taking a swig of beer. When she sees our faces, she knows we didn't react favorably to her comment. "Just kidding. You know I love my twin."

"I love you too," says Violet, sitting down at the table. "What are you saying about me now, Keely?"

"I was just responding to their question. They asked about your necklace."

Violet's face flushes hot. "I lost it."

"Well, *I* found it." Keely is such a smart ass. "It's in your jewelry box."

"Stay out of my things!" Violet says angrily. "You have no boundaries, Keely. Stay the hell out of my stuff." Without another word, Violet stands up, drops a twenty on the table, and leaves.

"Well, that went well," declares a belligerent Keely.

"Why do you do that?" Lainie asks, standing up. "Why do you try to rile her up all the time?"

"Because," Keely whines. "She never talks to me. Not anymore. We used to talk all the time. The more time that passes, the less we talk. We used to tell each other *everything*."

"She's just introspective," Lainie says, laying down her own twenty. "I'm going to follow her—make sure she's okay."

"I'll go too," says Keely, standing.

"No." Lainie sounds extra bossy. "Let me handle this."

"Fine," Keely mutters, adding, "She's *my* fucking twin."

I reach my hand out and place it on top of Keely's. "You are. But let Mama Lainie do her thing."

That makes Keely laugh. I guess she recovered quickly from Violet's outburst. "Mama Lainie? Wow, you nailed that. I wonder if Keeton calls her Mommy in bed." She throws her head back in a fit of hysterical laughter. When she finally calms a little, she finishes by slapping her hand on the table. "Oh, shit. That's funny stuff."

"Uh-huh," I mumble. "Funny." *Not.*

CHAPTER SEVENTEEN

Ian

IT'S BEEN four days since that night at Agatha's, and she still hasn't messaged me. No text. No voicemail. No nothing. So, while there's a part of me that's relieved by that, a bigger part of me is a little pissed. Why wouldn't she contact me? I'm working on clearing her name, for Christ's sake. Isn't she at least a little curious if I've found out anything? For all she knows, I could have broken the case wide open.

"Fuck." I'm definitely not happy about this turn of events. Fine. If she can't bring herself to call me, I'm not going to play these bullshit games. Sitting in my car on my way to grab lunch for Jason and myself, I decide to take the initiative——be the bigger man, or person, in this case.

Me: Hey, Agatha. What's up? It's me, Ian.

I stare at my phone for thirty seconds or so. *It's me, Ian? Can that sound any more pathetic?* When I see nothing happening, no response, I start up my sedan and head out to grab lunch. I let myself think about what I've learned in the last few days. "Nothing." Well, that's not true. Jason figured out that the software on Agatha's computer was most likely installed using that flash drive she found on her desk. From the lack of information on the server and cloud, he's confident that whoever installed the software used it to control Agatha's computer from a personal device of some sort. It could have even been a cell phone.

Jason was also able to pinpoint the times of day the transactions occurred. The billing and payments were consistent with regards to times of day. Like clockwork.

I snap my fingers. "I've got it." The excuse to call her. I need to ask her about those periods of time. There had to be a reason why the transactions always happened between ten thirty and ten forty-five in the morning. There was no deviation to those times. The only variation was the days of the month the invoices appeared and were paid. The only person who can speak to why that would be is Agatha.

At the sub shop, I decide to text her one more time, now that I have something to ask her.

Me: I've got a question about the timing of the transactions. Can you call me?

I don't have to wait this time. My phone rings. "Hello?"

"Hey, Ian. It's Agatha."

"Oh, hey. How you been?"

"Good."

Good? That's it? She's not going to ask me how *I* am? Rude. "I'm good too." I chuckle but get nothing from the other end of the line.

"You had a question for me?"

"I do, but I don't think I should ask you over the phone."

"Why not?" She sounds concerned. "Do you think I'm being bugged or something?"

No. I don't think she's being bugged, but I'll go with it. "You never know."

"Seriously?" she says, sounding even more distressed.

"Don't worry. I just like to play it safe. Why don't I stop over tonight? Bring some food."

"I can't tonight."

Why the hell not? "Oh? You've got plans?" *A date?*

"Yes."

Yes, what? What kind of plans? Shit, I can't ask her. It's none of my business. "Tomorrow night?"

"I'm not sure yet."

It *is* a date. "What about lunch tomorrow?"

I hear her sigh. "Just ask me over the phone. I find it hard to believe anyone cares who I talk to."

My turn to sigh. "Fine. Jason determined that all of the transactions occurred just after ten thirty in the morning. Is there any significance to that time?"

"Yes. That's when I took my break."

"Every day?"

"No. Not every day but close. You could set your watch by it, I guess you could say. I went down to get coffee at Java Jane's at that time."

"Every day," I repeat. "Every single day?"

"Yes. Every day. Unless I was in a meeting or something. That'd be the only reason I'd miss it."

"Wasn't that expensive?" Buying a fancy coffee every day really adds up.

"Well, I was in the Cuppa-the-Month program. Why are you asking about that? Do you think I embezzled money to support my coffee habit?" She's laughing, but it sounds hollow.

"No, I didn't mean anything by it. I've got my own coffee addiction. It's expensive. That's all."

"It's my only real indulgence. Or, it used to be."

I get that. Moving on. "Who knew about your routine? Did anyone ever go with you?" That could narrow down the field of mains.

"Why? Do you have a suspect?"

"I've got several."

"Like who?"

I sigh again. "This conversation would be better in person."

"Just give me one name. I bet I can help eliminate a suspect or two."

"Camille—"

"What?" she screeches in my ear. "No way! She's my best friend, Ian. She'd never...." Her voice goes quiet, then she says, "Wait! It can't be her because she used to go to break with me."

"Every day?"

"Most days. It was our girl talk time."

Hell, I don't even want to know what that means. "Fine. Let's assume that Camille isn't involved; who else knew your schedule? Who else went for coffee with you?"

"Trent. Sometimes."

Trent? "Alone?"

"Yes, but sometimes the three of us would go."

"How often?"

"How often what?"

"How often would you and Trent go alone?"

"Oh, um...." She sounds nervous. "Once or twice."

"A month?"

"No. A week."

She went out for coffee *once or twice* a week with Trent? "Were you seeing Trent? Romantically?"

"No. Of course not. We were just friends."

Why do I find that hard to believe? "Okay, for the sake of argument, let's say Camille and Trent aren't involved. If that's the case, who else would want to frame you? Kim?"

"I can't picture Kim doing anything like that. She's got her hands full with her daughter."

"Daughter? My background research on Kim didn't list any children."

"Well, that's because it's really her niece. Her sister died in an accident, and Kim was the only living relative."

"When did that happen?"

"A couple years ago."

"Why wouldn't that appear in the background check?"

"Her sister lived in California. Did you only check Arizona?"

I did only check Arizona and Nevada. "I'll check California. No matter, it still wouldn't preclude her from setting you up. It may give her even more reason to take the money. Kids are expensive."

"I thought the embezzlement started four years ago. If that's true, why would Kim need money for her niece prior to two years ago?"

True. Agatha's good at this. "Coincidence?" And instinct. Kim doesn't seem to like me very much, and I don't know why.

"Coincidence?" she chuckles. "There's no such thing."

"What about the fact her office is across from yours? She'd be able to keep an eye on you. She'd know when you were away from your desk." It'd be risky for the thief to assume she was gone at that time every single day. They'd need to have an eye on her. Which leads me to Kim.

"True, but Kim? That one doesn't feel right."

"Then who does?"

"That's just it, I can't think of anyone who'd want to do this to me. Well," she scoffs, "except for Drake. He hated me."

"Why do you say that?"

"Call it a hunch."

A hunch? She's not telling me something.

"I need to go, Ian. Can we talk about this later?"

"Sure, honey. We'll talk later."

"Okay. Have a good night, Ian."

Well, shit. "You too. Bye, Agatha."

"Bye."

YES, I know this is wrong, but I'm not doing it to be a creeper. I'm doing it to make sure she's safe. Following Agatha from her home all the way to Flagstaff sounds a bit crazy, but trust me, I've done worse. Try tracking a serial killer. Wow, that came out wrong. I'm not insinuating Agatha is in any way a serial killer. I *am* worried about her being out on her own. What if she actually encounters a serial killer?

What? It could happen.

It's almost dusk, which means soon, darkness will help obscure me. I stay back two or three cars once we get into Flagstaff city limits. I'm close enough to see when she turns. When she pulls into a hotel parking lot, I nearly choke. This *is* a date. She's meeting someone at a hotel, for fuck's sake. "Don't overreact, Burke."

As soon as she steps out of her car, I sigh in relief. She's wearing the same outfit she wore the night she broke into the H&S anniversary party. The only difference? She's not wearing a wig and she's got on flat shoes instead of heels. Agatha moves toward the back entrance of the hotel, where there's a truck with a logo on the side that reads Class Act Catering. The same company that worked the H&S party. "What are you doing here, Agatha?" I mutter to myself. Is she following another lead?

Instead of following her through the back, I decide to move to the front of the hotel. From there I should be able to inquire about any and all functions happening in their party rooms. At the front desk, I see small signs instructing visitors where various events are taking place. For example, the Johannes wedding reception is in the Concord Ballroom, while another sign lists a business meeting in Conference Room A.

My gut says she's working the wedding, so I start there. Following the signs to the space, I see the doors to the room are closed. Quietly, I pull the door open and peer inside. The room is quite large, and it's filled with white-linen-covered round tables. It looks like they each seat eight people. I quickly count the number. Twenty-five tables plus a head table for the bridal party. It reminds me of my own wedding. It was a similar setup, with most of the guests being agents and others who worked at the Bureau. The night was sort of a blur. Catherine planned the entire thing on her own. One of her complaints about me was my disinterest in wedding planning, something she reminded me of whenever possible.

In retrospect, Catherine and I were young. I was twenty-nine, she was thirty. Okay, so I guess we weren't *that* young. It's probably because at forty-one, I feel old as hell now, and my marriage seems like it was a million years ago. Honestly, I'm not sure why I did it. She was hot as fuck—the sexiest woman I'd ever met. Plus, she was a better shot than me. Hell, she was a better agent than me. I loved that about her. Until I didn't.

Shaking off those memories, I step into the room and slide to the left into a dark corner. From here, I'll be able to see if Class Act Catering is, in fact, working this event. It doesn't take me long to spot one of the crew in the same dark pants, white shirt, and red tie ensemble. "This is it," I say softly to myself. Scooting further into the corner, I do my best to blend into the background and watch the catering staff scurry around like mice in a cheese factory. *Mice in a cheese factory?* I chuckle to myself.

I'm about to change spots when someone hisses near my ear, "Ian!"

I jump. She snuck up on me like a little ninja. If I were still in the Bureau, I'd be fucking dead. Literally and figuratively. I'm losing my fucking touch. "Oh, hey there."

"What the hell are you doing here?" she snaps.

I stare down at her in her irate state. Her mouth is opening and closing like a fish's. Her little hands are clenched into mighty fists on either side of her hips, and I could swear she's tapping one foot on the ground. I want to laugh but she's seriously pissed. "Ian. I asked you a question. What. Are. You. Doing. Here? Are you following me?" She looks down at her feet for a second, adding, "I *knew* someone was following me from Page. It could *feel* it."

Might as well come clean. "That was me, yes." Fuck. I'm losing my touch. Have I said that already?

"Why?"

"You wouldn't tell me what you were doing. I was worried. I thought you were going to put yourself at risk again. Who're you looking for at this wedding, anyway?"

"At risk? Who am I looking for?" She sounds flabbergasted. "No one." She runs her palm over the top of her head. Looking back toward the others in her crew, she says, "I'm working."

"Working? As in working with the catering company?"

"Yes. She liked my work the other night." She gives me a small smile, then shrugs. "I need the money." She pauses again, then looks me in the eye. "Don't tell anyone. I'd like to keep this on the down low. I'm sort of embarrassed I've got to wait tables again like I did in high school and college. Not that it's a bad thing. I feel lucky to have a job at all. It's just... my life is regressing at a fantastical rate, and I'd prefer not to have to explain my predicament to anyone I know."

That was a lot to take in, but I've got to ask. "You're not here to investigate?"

She slowly shakes her head. "No. I'm just working, and I need to get back to it, which means you need to scram." She turns to walk away.

"Scram?" Jesus, I think this girl was born in the wrong decade.

"Yeah, you know what that means? It means Go. Home."

"Sure. Right. Yeah. I'll take off now that I know you weren't private dicking again."

Her face flushes to a hot pink. "I so regret saying that to you now."

With a chuckle, I say, "Oh, I don't. I haven't had this much fun in a long time." And that's abso-*fucking*-lutely true. This woman makes me smile. "Talk to you later?"

"Sure."

She probably assumes I mean in a day or two. *Not this time, sweet Agatha.* This time I plan on hanging back and making sure she's safe. Hell, I might even get a free dinner out of the deal. That'd be nice. I'm really tired of fast food.

CHAPTER EIGHTEEN

AGATHA

WHY IS HE HERE? Every time I turn around, he's there. I could have sworn I saw him talking to the bride and groom, and I *know* I saw him eating the steak option at table twenty. How is he getting away with that? Did he tell them he's a guest? A wedding crasher? A secret agent?

"Geesh," I say, wiping the sweat from my brow. We've just cleared the dessert dishes and now, while the best man and maid of honor give speeches, we'll be behind the scenes washing dishes, packing up, and loading the truck. I check my watch and wince. My feet hurt even though I'm wearing flats. I borrowed them from Sadie, but they hurt like a mo-fo. If I'm going to do this job for a while, I'm going to have to splurge and buy myself some black sneakers.

"Agatha?"

I turn to see Beth approach. "The drunken dancing has started, which means we can begin to clear the rest of the tables." We'd left water glasses and the dessert plates on the tables until they were finished. "Will you clear tables twenty through twenty-five?"

"Sure thing." I hope what's-his-name is gone now. Taking a large oval tray, I walk out the door and work my way around the ballroom until I'm at table twenty. He's still here. I don't know why I'm surprised. When he spots me, he smiles but doesn't engage, thank goodness. I unfold the metal tray stand that was leaning against one wall and set the large tray on top, then round the table, picking up small plates, silverware, and water glasses one by one. At Ian's spot, I reach out, leaning close to him. He smells nice. It's either cologne or manly soap. What-ever it is, it's musky and a little citrusy. Just as I'm about to take his water glass, he touches my wrist. I feel him lean toward me, and his breath tickles my ear as he says softly, "I'd like to keep that, please, beautiful."

I hesitate for a moment. My thoughts are all jumbled. Okay. First off, when he touched me just now, I felt a zing. That's not good. Secondly, he called me beautiful. That's bad too. *Be strong, Aggie.* I give myself a mental head slap. "The sooner we clear the tables, the sooner we're done," I say as quietly as I can without looking at him directly. I can't be this close to him *and* look at him.

"Fine." He pulls his hand away, and it makes me a little sad.

"You should go," I say next.

"No."

Standing upright, I look him right in his icy blue eyes. Gah! He's making me so mad. "Why not? I'm not going to embezzle cake," I snap.

Chuckling, he leans back in his chair while placing his hand on my lower back. Chills again, damn it. "I'm here until you're ready to go."

What? "Why?" I hiss.

Before he can answer, an older woman sitting on the other side of Ian interrupts. "Oh, Ian. Is this your young lady?"

I want to laugh. Young lady? But I don't get the chance because his hand wraps further around my waist, pulling me to him. "Yes, ma'am. This is my Agatha."

My Agatha!? What the heck? I know I looked shocked. I know it because my mouth is open so wide, I feel air at the back of my teeth.

"Call me Calliope, son."

"Calliope, meet my girlfriend, Agatha. Agatha, meet Calliope Fredrickson."

I reach my hand out to shake her outstretched one. She's a tiny woman, probably in her eighties. Her small hand is shaking slightly when I take it in mine. "Nice to meet you, ma'am."

She rolls her eyes. "So formal." When a smile crosses her lips, I smile back. "Isn't he a wonderful boyfriend? To stay here to keep an eye on you and make sure you get home safely?" Patting Ian's hand, she continues, "I'm so glad to hear chivalry isn't dead." Turning back to me, she says curtly, "I hope you appreciate what you have here, my dear. He's special."

"Oh, I do, ma'am. I sure do," I say as sweetly as I can. "Okay, sugarplum." I pat Ian's hand. "I've got to get back to work. I can't get fired. Who'd support us then?"

When I turn to walk away, I hear his rumbling laughter. "Good one, babe."

Babe? Oh, my lord. My life is officially in the Twilight Zone.

BY TWO IN THE MORNING, we're finally done, and I can barely walk. "I'm broken," I whine to myself as I trudge to my car. I'm going to fall asleep at the wheel. I know it.

"You're not broken."

I scream. Literally. "What the hell, Ian? You scared the crap out of me." He's leaning against my car, arms crossed in front of his wide chest, legs extended and crossed at his ankles. He looks casual, like his favorite thing to do is hang out in the parking lot behind the Ramada Inn.

Pushing himself up to standing, he gets close to me. "You're too tired to drive."

I know. "No, I'm not."

Ignoring my response, he holds up two fingers and says, "You have two choices."

I'd roll my eyes but I'm too exhausted and I'm pretty sure it'll hurt. "Uh-huh."

"We can either stay in the room I reserved here at the hotel, or—"

I start to sputter, but when he uses his long finger to move my bangs out of my eyes, I stop.

"Or I can drive you home in your car."

"That's not necessary. What about your car? I—"

"I'll get it tomorrow. Jason would love the chance to get out of the office for a while."

"I don't want to stay here." I can't afford it.

Holding out his palm he says, "Keys?"

I dig through my purse until I find them. "Fine. Whatever. I'm too tired to argue." I'm even too tired to question him about tonight. Well, almost too tired. After he unlocks the car, I slide into the passenger seat and moan. "Catering is not for the weak," I mumble.

"I bet. You were working your ass off in there."

I side-eyed him. "What in the heck did you tell the bride and groom? I saw you talking to them."

"I told them I was Calliope's date."

I snort with laughter. "And they believed you?"

"Sure." He shrugs. "Apparently, to them, she's eccentric Aunt Calliope. Of course she'd bring a young stud as her date."

That makes me giggle. "Young stud."

Whispering in my ear, he says, "Oh, sweet Agatha. If you only knew."

Ignoring the innuendo and the sexy shiver that just ran down my spine, I ask, "What'd you tell Calliope? I mean, no way she'd fall for that."

"The truth."

I laugh again. "That you were stalking your 'girlfriend,'" I say with air quotes, "like a creeper?"

"Not in so many words."

When he reaches out and sets his hand on my leg, right above my knee, I tense.

"Initially, when I first decided to follow you, I was trying to determine if you were going on a date."

"A date?" And why would that matter? Not that I'd go on a date. It's been so long, I wouldn't know what to do on a date.

"You said you had plans."

"You thought I was going on a date? What? Were you worried I was meeting up with a serial killer?"

He winces at that.

"Sorry. I didn't mean that like it sounded," I say softly.

"I know." He looks over at me, giving me a soft smile. "Truth?"

"Always."

"I was jealous."

I'm blinking furiously. "Jealous?"

He gives my knee a gentle squeeze. "Jealous."

Well, I'll be damned. Who-da-thunk? "You? B-b-but yo-you're..." I want to say he's way out of my league, that he's a 9.5 and I'm a 5, tops, but the words won't come out. Instead I blurt, "Old." *Oh, yeah. Great save, Agatha.*

Chuckling again, he slides his palm up my leg about three or four inches. "I know." Turning his head, he looks at me with a heated stare. "I think you'll learn to appreciate the fact that age has its benefits."

Melted. I just melted. Well, okay, my panties melted, and that's saying something. I was pretty sure those parts stopped working a long time ago. Apparently not. "Oh. Okay," I say breathlessly, giving myself away like an amateur.

When his hand slides up one more inch, then squeezes, I know that he knows. He's got me.

CHAPTER NINETEEN

Ian

SHE'S asleep before we leave the Flagstaff city limits. I knew she was exhausted. I watched her throughout the night. Every hour that passed, she worked slower and slower. I observed her attempting to stretch out her back and shoulders a time or two. When she leaned against the wall to rub her feet, I knew she was going to be hurting. Calliope was right—chivalry isn't dead, at least not as it relates to me and Agatha Palmer. I've accepted that I like her. *A lot.* Not only that, I need to protect her. Keep her safe. I'm not sure she isn't in danger, to be honest. Whoever framed her isn't going to appreciate getting caught.

After pulling into her driveway, I walk around the car, open her door, and place one arm under her legs and the other around her back. Lifting her, I watch her eyes flutter open. "Ian?"

"I'm here." Right where I want to be.

"Okay."

Taking three steps up to her front porch and the door, I

juggle her until I'm able to put the house key into the lock. With the door open, I step into her living room and place her on the sofa. Turning back to the door, I shut and lock it. Next, I turn on the lamp next to the couch and watch as her eyes open.

"Thanks, Ian," she says sleepily. "I'd probably be parked at a rest stop right now."

"You fell asleep before we left Flagstaff."

She stands and approaches me. "I appreciate it, stalker." She laughs in a tired, husky voice. Patting my arm, she says, "I'm going to bed. Feel free to crash on the couch. I'll drive you wherever tomorrow."

I reach out to touch her arm. She stops, turning to me. Tugging her closer to me, I slide my hand into her hair that's no longer pulled into a neat bun. Some has come out of the knot so now it's messy in a very sexy way. "Agatha," I whisper. With my hand behind her head, I lean down and kiss her lips softly. "Night, beautiful."

"Night, Ian."

I watch her walk away. She's unbuttoning her blouse as she walks. By the time she's crossed into her bedroom, it's slipping from her shoulders.

THIS IS the most uncomfortable couch ever built. It could be because I'm over six feet tall and the couch can't be more than five feet long. I'm curled into a ball, using a sofa pillow under my head and her small throw over my bare legs. I stripped down to my boxers before lying down because it's hot. Ordinarily, I sleep in the buff. I didn't think that would fly here at Chez Agatha.

Throwing back the thin blanket in frustration, I move to sitting. Placing my head in my hands, I sigh loudly.

"Can't sleep?" Her voice is husky from sleep.

I jump at her words. I didn't hear her approach. I swear I've lost my touch around this woman.

"Yes." I look up at her. She's wearing one of those night-gowns that covers her entire body. Why is that sexy? "No." I chuckle. "This couch was made for someone much smaller than me."

I watch as she taps her little foot on the floor. She's wringing her hands like she's nervous. "You could sleep with me," she squeaks. "It's more comfortable than the sofa."

I stare into her eyes as she does her best to avoid looking into mine. "You sure?" I ask softly.

She nods, turning on her heel, she walks back toward her bedroom. I quickly follow her and watch her as she slides beneath the covers.

Looking down at her in her queen-size bed, I can't help noticing how pretty she is. Like an angel. Pulling back the covers on the opposite side, I slide onto the cool, soft cotton and sigh. "That's what I'm talkin' about."

Fluffing up the pillow, I roll to my side so that I'm facing her back. The minute I'm comfortable, Agatha rolls over, facing me. "Ian?"

"Yeah, honey."

God, she's sweet.

And soft. Did I mention soft? I know this because she's scooted her body toward mine until our legs and arms are touching. Wrapping her arm over my shoulder, around my neck, she pulls closer.

"Fuck," I mutter. My dick likes this position. A lot.

"Mm," she says in a sleepy voice. "Ian," she whispers as she presses her cheek to mine. "You smell so good."

Fuck.

"Kiss me," she whispers.

So, I do. I fucking do. I use my tongue to nudge her lips open. *Let me in, Agatha.* She responds perfectly. Beautifully. Our tongues meet in a slow, sexy caress. My hand slides down from the top of her back, down, down, until my palm is cupping her luscious ass. I squeeze one cheek, pulling her closer to me. My cock is so damn hard it's trying to break free from my boxers. It's then I think, *What the hell are you doing, Burke?*

AGATHA

MY BODY IS ON FIRE. I feel hands everywhere—on my ass, on my nipple, and one palm is sliding beneath my nightgown. *Oh, my God. This is amazing.* I roll my hips toward the feeling, attempting to get the ache to stop. "I feel so achy," I hear myself whine.

A deep voice whispers in my ear, "I've got you, honey."

Ooh, my dream man has a deep, sexy voice. Arching into the touch, I feel something hard against my stomach. When fingers slide into my panties, I freeze. It's been ages since someone other than myself has touched me there. When he pinches my nipple, I moan. I can't help it. You would too. His thick fingers are doing amazing, magical things to my clit. Things no one has ever done. Not even me.

"Ian?" I squeak.

"Yeah, honey?"

Oh, shit. I should stop him. I really should. How did it even get to this point? I squeeze my eyes closed tightly, focusing all my attention on the sensations he's giving me.

"Put your leg over my hip, sweetheart."

Instead of doing what I should—you know, jumping up and stopping this insanity—I do it. I lift my left leg and place it onto his hip. It opens me up for him.

"This okay, Agatha?" he whispers in my ear.

"Yesss," I hiss as his finger moves to my center. "Don't stop."

"You're so fucking wet, honey."

I love that endearment—*honey*. And I *am* so damn wet. I don't ever remember being this turned on in my life. Neither of my college boyfriends knew what they were doing, but I get the distinct impression that this man does. "Oh, God." I moan as he wiggles his fingers inside me and around my clit. My nipple is getting a workout as well. When his mouth starts to nibble and lick my neck, just below my ear, it's over. "I'm coming," I pant.

"Shit, sweetheart. You're squeezing the hell out of my fingers." He kisses my neck again, then bites the lobe of my ear, and I squeak; he chuckles.

When I start to come down from the high of my orgasm, I stiffen. Probably not as stiff as the long, hard thing poking me but still pretty stiff. As nonchalantly as possible, I roll away from him to quickly move off the bed to standing. "Ian. I...."

He's got that expression on his face—half grimace, half smile. I watch him as he discreetly wipes his hand on his stomach. Oh, my God. His stomach. It's flat and it looks hard. Damn, he's got a great body.

Rolling onto his back, he runs his big palms over his face. I blush, thinking about him doing that with my, um, me all over his hand. I'm distracted by the tent in his boxers. It looks like it'd sleep a family of six.

I'm still gazing unabashedly at his crotch when he says, "Agatha?"

"Huh?" I reply, still staring.

Chuckling, he places his palm over it. "Agatha?"

Busted. "What? Huh?" I shake my head slightly and look at his face finally. "Sorry." My face heats to about a million degrees.

"I'm sorry." Carefully, Ian sits up. "I shouldn't have—"

"No, it's okay."

He arches his brow. "Should I have stayed on the sofa?"

"No. It was, er, it is. It's okay." Stepping closer to the bed, I place my palm on his shoulder to reassure him. "Ian, I'm a grown woman. You're a grown man. We're two consenting adults. I'm fine. Better than fine." I smirk. "But, how are you?" I ask, nodding down toward his still tented boxers.

"I'll be fine. Just stop looking at him. He likes you."

Oh, my. Did he just say that? I giggle nervously. It feels good to laugh. I haven't had much to laugh about lately. I needed that. *All of it.*

Ian slides out of bed and excuses himself to the bathroom. He's in there for a while. I'd like to know what he's doing, but it's none of my business. When he steps out of the bathroom, I see he's back to normal—you know, in the penis department. I blush again thinking of it. And by "it" I mean his *it.*

"Stop blushing. You're giving me a complex." His laughter rumbles as he slides beneath my sheets.

"Sorry." Not sorry.

"It's still too early to call Jason. He'll kill me if I wake him up at this hour. Let's get some sleep, honey."

I WAKE up alone and sit up quickly. Was it all a dream? Ian in my bed? Ian touching me, kissing me? When I hear someone out in my main room, I smile. "He's still here," I whisper. Lying back onto my pillow, I snuggle into the sheets, remembering the night before. My body's still sore from the wedding, but I'll live. Especially now that I've got this sexy man in my life.

But is he in my life? Are we a thing? A couple? It certainly seemed that way in the car. Not to mention in my bed. A shiver runs through me, thinking about his big, warm hands all over me. It's like nothing I've ever experienced. No man has ever taken control and given me such pleasure. Not my two college boyfriends, and definitely not the one-night stand I had in Vegas a couple years ago. That guy knew what he was doing, until he passed out, but it's nothing like Ian. I guess he was right, what he said in the car: *I think you'll learn to appreciate the fact that age has its benefits.*

Now, my question is, how good is he at the rest of it? I shiver again, recalling how big he felt. How hard. "I bet he's an amazing lover," I whisper.

Rolling out of bed, I pull my fuzzy blue robe off the hook on the back of my door, slide it over my shoulders, and tie the belt tightly around my waist. In the kitchen, I see the coffee brewing and two mugs sitting next to it. He must have just gotten up. Looking around the room, I note the time on the stove. "Almost nine." Shoot, I bet he's late. I scan the living room and see the front door is ajar. He must have stepped outside. No wonder, it's supposed to be a beautiful morning. I wish I had a patio in the back. That'd be the perfect spot for morning coffee with Ian while we read the paper—solve the crossword puzzle together. At least I've got that cute little sitting area on my front porch.

Rolling my eyes at my stupid, romantic thoughts, I fill both cups with coffee. I wonder how he takes his? Deciding to find out, I step toward the door but stop when I hear Ian's voice. He must be on the phone. Not wanting to eavesdrop, I take one step back until I hear him say my name. Is he calling for me or talking about me? Moving closer to the opening, I press my ear to the door. Yes, I know it's wrong, but the man is talking about me. Maybe he's talking to his mom. If so, he could be telling her he's met "the one." I'd snort, but I need to stay quiet. Just know, the snort was internal. Moving my ear closer, I hear him.

"No, of course not. Nothing's going on. You wanted me to find the money, right?"

There's silence. I hold my breath, waiting for him to say more.

"Of course. That's exactly what I'm doing. You don't think she'd tell me if she thought I was the enemy, do you?" He laughs, and it's a hard, callous laugh. I hate it. I hate everything about this conversation. It hurts. It hurts everywhere. Especially my heart. This whole thing was a ruse. A ruse to get stupid, pathetic Agatha to show him where that money is hidden. Well, ha! The joke's on him, because I have no idea where that money is.

"You hired me to do a job. I'm doing it. I don't need you dictating how it's done. I've still got almost forty days to—"

He doesn't finish. The other person, most likely Drake, must be talking.

"Let me do *my* job. I'll call *you* when I've found your money."

Yep. It's got to be Drake.

I hear Ian mutter, "Fuck."

I move away from the door. Scampering back to the kitchen, I pretend pour our coffee since I already did it, humming as I do. Humming is difficult because all I want to do is throw his ass out and then throw myself onto my bed so I can cry in peace.

When he comes up behind me, he wraps his cold, dead hands around me, kissing the back of my neck. I shiver, but it's not in a good way. "Thanks for making the coffee," I squeak. "How do you take yours?" *Like I give two shits.*

"Black."

Like his heart.

"*Welp!* Here you go, sir." I start to hand him the cup, then hold it back. "Wait, I bet you'd like it to go, right? It's late. You probably need to get to work. Do you want me to drive you or is Jason picking you up?" I set both cups down. "Let me run in and get dressed. I'll drive you."

I haven't stopped talking, and he hasn't said a word. Racing into my bedroom, I pull open the drawer that houses my loungewear. Sliding on a pair of black yoga pants, I move to my closet to get a sweatshirt. I'm dressed in less than two minutes. I run a brush through my hair quickly and pull it back into a messy bun. Locating my glasses on a side table, I slide those on along with a pair of flip-flops that are sitting by the door. Bam. Ready to go. Lickety-split.

When I step back into the main room, I search for my purse and keys. Ian drove my car so I need to find where he left my keys before we can go. I'm about to ask him where they are when I notice he's looking through the things on my table. The place I set up as my investigation station. Ooh, that rhymes. I like the sound of it. What I don't like is him snooping through my things. "What are you doing?"

Without looking up, he asks, "Did you have your laptop open last night?"

"No." I haven't used that for several days. I've been crazy busy.

He turns to face the front door. Then he moves to stand next to the couch as he stares at his phone. Turning back toward me, he points toward the table. "Did you move the table?"

"No. Ian. What's this about?"

He mumbles or hums something, returning to the table. When he begins to lift things off the table one at a time, I can't take it. "Look. I think you need to go."

"Hm-hmm. Jason's on his way."

Thank goodness.

He's still moving everything on my table, setting things on the chair after he's looked at them from all sides. Even the papers. "Ian?"

"Shh," he says rudely.

When he picks up my *Aggie Palmer* nameplate, it's the last straw. I've had just about enough. "No, *you* shush. This is *my* house." Reaching out, I yank the object out of his hand so hard it slips out of mine and flies backward, hitting the wall. I look back and see the silver plate has separated from the wooden base. "See what you made me do?" I stomp over to it. Bending down, I pick up the plate, then the wooden base. As I do, I spy small wires poking out from inside the hollowed-out wood base. "What's this?"

Ian is next to me in a flash. "Let me see."

Yeah, I know I'm mad, sad, and all that, but I'm out of my league with whatever this thing is.

I hand it over and watch as he holds it up to the light. The plate is opaque, solid—except for the dot on the *i* in Aggie. It's not solid. It's a tiny, pin-size hole. A hole with light shining through it. I watch as he sets that down so he can resume checking out whatever is inside the base.

"Ian? What is it?"

"A camera."

"A what?" I screech. "A camera?"

Turning to me, he looks into my eyes. "Similar to a nanny cam. Agatha, tell me about this thing. Was this on your desk at work?"

"Yes."

"Okay. Did you buy it?"

"No. It was a gift."

"From who?"

I shrug. "Secret Santa. I don't know who gave it to me."

"How long ago was that?"

"Four or five years ago."

"So, this was on your desk at work. It's been there for four or five years?"

Duh, I just said that. I nod slowly. "Yes."

"This," he points at the tiny camera, "is how they knew when you were at your desk and when you weren't."

"They?"

"Whoever took the money."

Okay, that reminds me. "You just told whoever you were talking to that you were trying to trick me. Are you saying you believe me?"

Pulling his phone out of his pocket, he clicks some keys. Turning the screen to face me, I see a grainy image of me and Ian kissing. I stare at the image. I recognize my living room, my sofa. My front door is in the background of the picture. "I don't understand. Why do you have this?"

I vaguely remember a kiss last night. Was that from then? If so, "How?"

Ian points to the nameplate. "Whoever has control of that thing took a photo of us and sent it to Drake. I had to say those things to him to protect you." He pauses. "And me."

"Is that *thing* still working?" I move closer to the wooden base. "So, they've been watching me? In my home?" Shit, I've walked around naked more than once. Don't judge. I live alone. "Is there audio?" I like to sing. I *can't* sing. Like at all. It's enough some creeper saw me naked. If they heard me too, that'd be too embarrassing.

"Good question." Picking the name plate back up, he asks, "I assume it works using Wi-Fi and Bluetooth. Do you have wireless internet?"

I shake my head. "My neighbor does." I know I look guilty. I should. "I borrow his now and then."

"Honey, you need a secure Wi-Fi connection, but we can talk about that later." He turns, looking for something. Ah, his shoes. He slips them on and then holds up the wooden object. "Can I take this with me?"

"Are you going to show Jason?"

"Nope. Taking it to Phoenix. Some of our tech people will have to take a look at it. I'd like to know if there's audio too. If so, they've heard us talking. We could have shown our hand."

Our hand. *Our* hand. "So," I pause. "Was that Drake on the phone?"

Running his free hand through his salt-and-pepper hair, he says, "It was."

"He sent you the photo?"

"Yes."

"How did he get it?"

"He said someone sent it to him."

"Well, if you ask me, that's where you need to start. Find out who sent him the picture. Then you've got your man." I pause. "Or woman."

I watch as his face lights up. "That's absolutely right, Agatha." Moving to me, he wraps one arm around my neck and pulls me in. He kisses me lightly and then steps back. "You should be a private dick. You've got the knack."

I slap him on his chest and step away from him. "So, what you said to Drake about me? It's not true?"

"Honey." He steps closer. "It's not true. I like you."

What does that even mean? I like peanut butter. It's like the most mundane thing you can say to someone you just slept with. If he says the word *friend* in the next minute, I may punch him right in the kisser. I remain silent in the hopes he elaborates.

Ian's closing in on me. He slides his hand against my neck again until he's cupping my cheek. It feels good.

"I like you a lot. I liked what we did last night. But..."

Oh, here we go. "But?"

"But, it's complicated."

"Uh-huh." I step away from his touch. Holding up my palm in the universal halting gesture, I say, "Right. Complicated. Say no more." I walk into my kitchen and search a drawer. Finding what I need, I hand Ian a plastic Ziploc baggie.

"What's that for?"

"Evidence." I nod down at the spy camera.

"Right," he chuckles.

Okay. Now he's laughing at me? Making fun? "Well, this was fun, but I need to get on with my day." *My life.* I move toward my bedroom. "You can show yourself out, Mr. Burke."

"Agatha." He says my name like it's a statement, not a question. That means I don't need to answer. I move into my bedroom, shutting the door and locking it. Flopping onto my bed, I listen. Minutes later, I hear the front door open. "Lock up behind me, Agatha," he says loudly enough for me to hear.

"Sure thing, Mr. Complicated," I say, only loud enough for *me* to hear.

The front door shuts, and I take the time I need to feel sorry for myself. In case you were wondering, it took hours. Hours and some double chocolate chip ice cream, and a heart-to-heart phone call with my sister, Lainie. She always knows best.

CHAPTER TWENTY-ONE

Ian

WHEN I STEP out the door of Agatha's house, Jason's parked on the street. The expression on his face says all I need to know about Jason's mood. He's pissed. I texted him early this morning to come get me. If he's angry about that, wait until he hears he has to drive me back to Flagstaff to get my car. I chuckle to myself as I open the door. Maybe the Bluetooth camera we found this morning will improve his mood.

"Thanks for picking me up, man."

"Uh, huh. I don't even want to know what the fuck you're up to man. That right there," he nods at Agatha's house, "is a bad idea."

I know.

Holding up the baggie that contains the hollow wooden stand, I say, "Look what I found."

Jason takes the camera from me, pulling the bag tight so he can see the contents. He moves it around until he is able to see the entire device. Looking up at me, he chuckles, "This is nanny cam shit." He smirks, adding, "Start from the beginning."

It takes us after we've stopped for breakfast and made it to Flagstaff to work through the entire scheme.

"It's so simple, it's genius," says Jason as he pulls alongside my car. "Agatha's right, in a sense. If I can figure out who sent the picture, we've got our man. Or woman. However..." he pauses. He's about to blow Agatha's theory out of the water. "This person isn't stupid. They would have sent the image from someplace either untraceable or public, like the library."

"Do it anyway. See if you can find out where it came from. In the meantime, I'm heading to Phoenix to see if Basil can find out more about this." Holding up the camera, I open the door to step out.

"Basil's a twat," he grumbles.

Leaning back into the car, I ask Jason, "Someone had to order this thing. Can you see if you can find out who sold this specific device?"

"I'll see what I can find."

"I'll be back tonight."

"Why would you drive two hours to Phoenix, then over two hours back to Page when you could sleep in your own bed in your own home?"

I provide my own smirk. "I've got my reasons."

"You and your pussy. I swear, I can't believe how often you get it, old man."

I don't bother responding. When he referred to Agatha as mere *pussy*, I wanted to punch his smug-ass face. I slam his car door and walk to mine. The sooner I get this to Basil, the sooner I can be back to check on Agatha. She shouldn't be left alone.

～

AT PRECISELY EIGHT O'CLOCK, I'm standing on Agatha's front porch. I've knocked several times, but to no avail. Her house is dark, but her car is here. "Where are you, Agatha?" Only one way to find out.

Me: Agatha? Are you home?
Agatha: Nope.
Me: Where are you?
Agatha: Out

Out? On a date? No, she wouldn't be on a date. We talked about this. Right? Shit, I hate this. This feeling that I need to know what she's doing and hoping she's not doing it with another man.

Me: You're a very frustrating woman. I'm standing on your porch.
Agatha: I'm out. I'll talk to you tomorrow or the day after.

Or the day after? She's blowing me off. And not in a good way.

Me: Sure. Talk to you tomorrow. I've got some questions for you so the sooner the better.
Agatha: ...

She's about to type something, so I wait.

Agatha: Breakfast?
Me: I'll bring bagels.
Agatha: Yum. C U then.

I check my watch again. 8:05. I drove like a bat out of hell to get the camera to Basil. When he had it, he worked fast since he was familiar with the device. With one look, he could tell there wasn't a microphone as part of the device, which is good. The bad news? He didn't think he'd find much because it's a commonly used small camera found online. But he said he'd take a look anyway. After that, I went to my place, showered, packed up some clean clothes, and jumped back into my car. I've eaten only fast food today, so I feel like shit. That's why I picked up grilled chicken salads for Agatha and me. I guess I should have told her I'd be back tonight. I assumed she'd be here.

Sliding my phone back out, I send a text to Jason.

Me: Wanna get a beer?
Jason: Hellz yeah, old man.

He needs to stop calling me that. I'm getting a complex.

Me: Where?
Jason: Murphy's. You in town now?
Me: Yep
Jason: Meet you there in ten.
Me: Yep

I slide the phone back into my pocket. Holding up the bag with the food, I'm tempted to leave it on her front step for her to eat, but that could draw some unwelcome critters to her doorstep, so I toss it into the back seat of my sedan. If I'm going to Murphy's, I'm eating wings. I'll eat healthy tomorrow.

CHAPTER TWENTY-TWO

AGATHA

"AGGIE, there's an old guy staring at you."

I look at Keely, then follow her line of sight toward the bar. As discreetly as possible, I check to find that, in fact, a man *is* staring at me. A man I know intimately. "Ian," I grumble. *What's he doing here?* Following me, no doubt. The man is a certifiable stalker.

I lean over to whisper to Keels, "I know him."

"He's kind of hot for an old guy. Um—"

"He's not that old." And he is, in fact, hot. "Too bad he's—"

"Too bad I'm what?" asks the sexy, smirky man.

"I was about to tell you that he was walking this way, Aggs," Keely says, looking contrite.

I'm not going to finish what I started to say. "Well, well, well, if it isn't Mr. Complicated," I say without looking up. Instead I sip the golden beer from my glass. Sarcasm. It's the best.

Ignoring said sarcasm, Ian says, "You could have told me you were here."

"Why? I'm out with my sisters. Girls' night. Enjoying a nice local brew. Speaking of... nice seeing you, Ian. Have a good night."

He chuckles, and it makes my entire body tingle. *Stop it, you damn traitorous body.*

"Who are you?" asks Andrew, Sadie's boyfriend.

I guess it's not *technically* girls' night, but you know what I mean.

Ian looks at me expectantly. So, I give him what he wants. "This is Ian Burke. He's working for H&S to find the money I supposedly stole."

Ian smiles at Andrew and nods to my sister, Sadie. "I've gained five pounds thanks to your baked goods."

Sadie chuckles. "Good. Serves you right for investigating my sweet sister." Sadie turns away to talk to someone else.

"Ian Burke?" asks Lainie, taking charge. "How can we help you today?"

"I just stopped by to say hello."

"Well, hellooooo ladies," says another man as he throws his arm around Ian's shoulders. "I'm Jason. I work with this old guy." He turns to Lainie. I watch his eyes grow round, then narrow into a steely gaze that I'm assuming is supposed to be sexy but isn't. He's checking her out. Leaning toward my oldest sister, he coos, "Well, hello there, beautiful."

I hear Keely giggle.

"Um, hello yourself," replies Lainie.

"What's your name?" Jason asks as he slithers closer to her.

"*Mine*," says a deep, growly voice. Keeton Gustafson, Lainie's big, bad, biker boyfriend, reaches our table with a fresh pitcher of beer. "Step away," he adds, sounding not the least bit friendly.

With his hands up, Jason takes one step back. "No problem, man. There's lots more to choose from." Without taking a breath he continues, "I don't ever remember seeing a table full of such hot girls before, do you, Ian?"

"You did *not* just say that," mutters Sadie.

"He did," Violet replies. It's nice to hear her speak, since she hasn't said much tonight. "He called us girls and insinuated that he can just choose one of us." Vi's making up for her silence. It makes me smile.

"Ladies, I meant no disrespect. Right, bro?" He slaps Ian's back like he's expecting to get some backup.

We all turn to look up at Ian and watch as he rolls his eyes. It's funny and unexpected. So much so, everyone at the table laughs. Everyone except Jason.

Placing his hand on the back of Jason's neck, he nudges him away from our table. "Come on, Romeo, let's go. Our wings are getting cold."

"B-but—" Jason whines.

Ian ignores him, turning back toward me. Leaning down to whisper in my ear, he says, "I'm coming over tonight. We need to talk."

Oh, shit. I thought we were having breakfast. And that statement right there? Hit me right in the panties. *Double-crossing panties.* My turn for the old eye roll. "Whatever."

AS VIOLET APPROACHES MY HOUSE, I spot the dark sedan parked at my curb. Ian. When he left, he and I looked at each other and he gave me a sexy chin lift. I knew he'd be here just like he said. *God, this is such a bad idea.* I decide not to say a word to my sister; instead, I hop out of her car, thank her for being the designated driver, and speed walk to my front door, because maybe, just maybe, if I hurry, I can get into the house, lock the door, and pretend I'm not home.

No such luck.

"Agatha."

I don't see him, but I know he's sitting in the shadows of my front porch. It was the main selling feature of my little bungalow. The front porch spans almost the entire width of the front of the house. I've got a cozy seating area on one side with a fern and rug. I read out there when the weather is right. He must be in one of my wicker chairs. It's too dark to say for sure. He approaches me from the shadows, looking amazing in his tee and jeans.

I was too nervous at the bar to notice what Ian was wearing. Now that it's just the two of us, and thanks to the glow of my front porch light, I can really appreciate his attire. His jeans hug his thighs nicely. The legs taper down but not too much. Then there's his tee. It's heather gray and snug on his body. I didn't notice it at the bar, but I see it now. The front has small text in black that reads *Mischief Managed*.

That's it, put a fork in me, I'm done. He's wearing a Harry Potter tee. A tee I want to touch, badly. I'd bet anything it's soft.

"That's really creepy, Ian. I bet you were an excellent FBI agent. You know how to hide in plain sight."

"Actually, I was just so-so."

Just so-so? "Really?"

He stops in front of me and looks down at my face. "Really. If you fuck up and get sliced and diced by a serial killer, you're a pretty shitty agent."

"I'm sure the circumstances were beyond your control." I don't know why I'm trying to give him excuses. I wasn't there. Maybe he was a shitty cop.

"That's the thing," he says as he slides his finger down my cheek, pushing a rogue strand of hair out of my face. "I was trained to know how to handle exactly those situations and I fucked up."

"How?" I ask softly, because his hand feels nice now that it's moving up and down my arm.

"The Bureau had worked on the setup for weeks. We had agents, couples, at every city park in Chicago, because all of our intel told us the Slasher was going to strike that night and we knew that's where he liked to attack. My ex-wife and I were one of those couples. The plan was we'd be sitting on a park bench, making out like horny teenagers while other agents monitored us."

Ian hesitates, so I wait for him to continue.

"The Slasher came from out of nowhere. We didn't see him approach. My ear piece malfunctioned so I didn't hear warning from the team. We fucked up." He steps back, leaning against the side of the house. "I saw only a glint from his knife blade as it moved toward my wife. I had no time to draw my weapon. I only had time to react, pushing her down as I covered her body so I could take the brunt of the attack."

"You saved her life?"

Ian makes a scoffing sound. "I did, but that's not how she saw it."

"What do you mean?"

"Let's go inside." He nods toward my door. "I'll finish the story in there."

I take the key out of my front pocket and unlock the door. Pushing it open, I let Ian walk in first. He turns on a lamp I've got on a side table and moves to sit on the sofa. "Would you like something to drink? I've got water and wine."

"A glass of wine, actually. Thanks."

Me too. I pour us both a glass. I sit next to him and hand him his drink. "Keep going."

Leaning back, he sighs, "She saw it as a slight. Catherine

was working toward a promotion. She thought I sabotaged her entire career when I threw my body over hers to protect her."

Catherine. His wife's name was Catherine. "Did you?"

"No." He chuckles, but it's not funny. "My first instinct is to protect. I would have done the same thing to any partner I was working with, man or woman."

I place my hand on his leg, right above his knee. He notices. "I've only known you a short time, Ian, but I believe that about you." Gah! He's getting to me. I can feel his emotions all around us. I can tell this is hard for him to talk about. The fact that he's telling *me* means something. But my inner dialogue isn't going to let me off that easy. *Stop it right now, Agatha! Don't read too much into it. He's complicated, remember?*

"Thank you," he whispers.

Shoot. I'm getting the *feelz* again. "Is that why you retired?"

"Like I mentioned the other day, it was either that or sit at a desk. To become a pencil pusher. I would have gone batshit crazy at a desk all day. No offense."

"None taken. I get it. There were days as an accountant I just wanted to bolt. I think that's why I had my coffee shop breaks. I needed to get up and out of the office."

He leans forward to get his wine. I watch as he places the glass to his lips to sip. He's got sexy lips. "You're staring, Agatha."

I am. "No, I'm just thinking."

"About your failed FBI agent?"

My failed FBI agent? "No. What happened to Catherine? Did she get a promotion?"

"Yep."

"And you two couldn't work it out?" *What the heck am I doing?* This is none of my business.

"No. She said she'd never forgive me. That I was a misogynist."

"A misogynist? Why? Because you tried to save her life?"

He pauses, adding, "She spread the rumor that I said women should be at a desk, not out in the field which is fucking ridiculous. Plus, she was sleeping with our deputy director."

"She cheated?" God, I hate cheaters.

Nodding, he replies, "She did, and yes. Because I saved her life. She said she didn't need to be protected and that she would have gotten the Slasher if it weren't for me." Sipping his drink again, he sets it down, leans forward, places his palm on my cheek, and kisses me.

I guess he's done talking. I pull away from his soft, gentle kisses. "Ian?"

"It's been a long day, honey. I just want to slide into bed with you, wrap my arms around you, and sleep. We can finish talking tomorrow. Yeah?"

He wants to slide into bed with me? Wrap his arms around me? My neglected lady parts are screaming, *hellz yeah!* But the realist in me knows I shouldn't. This is a terrible idea. But I want it. Even though it's a very bad idea, even though he's complicated. This, whatever this is, will never last. I know it, and so does he. I'm going to get hurt. But the truth is, I crave his touch.

"Yeah."

He stands up first, holding his hand out to me. Placing mine in his big, warm one, I stand and lead the way to my bedroom. My mind races. What should I wear to bed? My nightie is hanging on the hook with my robe. I wore that last time. Instead, I step to my dresser and withdraw a tee and shorts. He's watching me. "I'll, uh, just change in the bathroom."

"Sounds good."

I race out the door and down my short hallway into my bathroom. I quickly change into my sleepwear, brush my teeth and hair, use the facilities, and remove the little remaining makeup on my face. "This is a bad idea, Agatha." It is, but my entire life has been safe. I don't remember the last time I did anything risky. Well, the guy in Vegas. That was certainly risky, and fun—until the guy suddenly started snoring. This is different. For one, we're both sober—sort of. For another, I'm tired of being risk-averse. No, this time I'm doing it. I'm climbing into bed with the sexiest guy I've ever met. Some fooling around would do me good.

Standing next to my bed, I see Ian's already undressed. His shirt is off, but the sheet and blanket are covering his lower half, so I don't know if he's naked. Sliding beneath the covers, I lie stiffly, like a mummy in a tomb.

"Relax, Agatha," he whispers in my ear. His arm reaches across me, nudging me until I'm facing him. "Tell me more about Kim Reynolds."

Oh, so we're talking about this now? So much for fooling around. "What about her?" He can't possibly think Kim did this.

"You've worked with her for six years?"

"About, yeah."

"What's she like?"

"Nice. Quiet. We got along well. We weren't close or anything. We didn't socialize."

"Did she have other friends at work?"

"Ian, you can't possibly think Kim would do this. She's trying to make a home for her daughter."

"She's single, right?"

"She is now. The guy she was with didn't want kids, so they split up when she got Amelia."

"That's pretty shitty. He sounds like an ass."

"He was in law enforcement." I smirk, but he misses it since it's pretty dark in the room.

"Oh? Now that makes sense. Was he a federal agent?"

"Not sure. Camille would probably remember. I could ask her. What makes sense?"

"She knew about the Slasher and my wife. Ex-wife. So, what about Monica Bellamy?"

Changing the subject, I see. "No way. She's a sweetheart. She'd never—"

"Agatha, trust me when I say that criminals can take on a role, act the part. We're talking about your freedom, honey. You can't trust anyone."

Not even you? "My freedom? What're you talking about? I thought they weren't going to press charges."

Rubbing his hands over his face, he releases a deep breath. "They told you it was over one hundred thousand, yeah?"

"Yes."

"But you know it was actually over a million, right?"

I nod. "Yes." *I'm not going to like this.*

"Once we find the rest of the money, they intend to press charges."

Sitting up ramrod straight, I sputter, "B-b-but I didn't take the money. What if whoever did this created more accounts in my name?"

Ian wraps his arm around me, pulling me into his chest. "Shush. We'll figure it out." His palm is rubbing my back, up and down. It feels good. "I promise, baby, we'll figure it out."

"Okay," I say weakly. "I feel so pathetic and worthless. I can't really help."

"You're not worthless *or* pathetic. You're helping more than you know. Now, tell me about Monica, then Trent."

Trent? He suspects Trent?

"I've had drinks with Monica a few times. I know she's married with a couple of kids. She's got their pictures on her desk. They're really cute."

"Good. Great information, Agatha. Do you think her kids

could be involved?" he chides. His question is light, there's humor in his voice.

I laugh and slap his bare chest lightly. "Fine. Let's see, they've got a nice-ish house. She's worked at H&S for four or five years."

"Five."

"Okay, five. But that's really all I know. I told you she was funny."

"Monica Bellamy is funny. Got it."

Ignoring the smart-ass comment, I move on to Trent. "Trent. He's been there a long time. I'm not sure how long. He's single..." *and ready to mingle. Snort.* "He was always nice. To me, anyway."

Ian stops rubbing my back. It's like he freezes. "You have feelings for Trent?"

"What?!" I squeak. "No. We were just..."

"Friends?"

"Yes, Ian. Just friends."

"But you wanted more?"

"No. Not really." And I think I mean that. Trent was just a fixation. If I'd really wanted something with him, I'm pretty sure I would have done something about it. "No. I didn't want more."

"Are you trying to convince yourself or me?"

Why does he sound angry?

"There was never anything there. We were just friends. He was kind to me. We had coffee and lunch sometimes. He'd join our group when we went out for drinks. That's it."

"Mm-hmm." Ian slides back down beneath the covers. "I'm beat, honey. In the morning, I want to ask you about Drake and—"

I growl.

"You don't care for Drake?"

"Nope. You want talk about Drake and who else?"

"Miriam."

"Miriam Smith? Ha! That's a joke. There's no way she could pull off a computer scheme like that. Not without help. She's computer illiterate. According to Trent, that IT guy, Victor, is in her office almost daily trying to help her with stuff. Hell, Camille's even tried to help her with stuff." I laugh but it comes out more pig-like. Snorting isn't the most attractive sound.

"That's interesting. Victor Smiley?"

"That's the one."

"I've met Victor."

I shiver. "Victor always gave Camille and me the willies."

"How so?"

"Well, for me, it was because he believes showering is optional, but Camille said his eyes were super pervy, and she claimed he was always grinning at her when no one else was looking."

"He does have an odor, and as for the grin, isn't his last name Smiley?"

"Ha! Funny man."

He yawns and moves in closer, wrapping his arms around me. "We'll finish up in the morning."

"You were going to bring bagels," I whine.

"I'll still get you bagels, baby," he whispers in my ear sweetly.

Gah! Why, why, why am I letting this man in when I know all he's going to do is ransack my heart?

CHAPTER TWENTY-THREE

Ian

Victor Smiley
>Age: 57
>DOB: 3-17-61
>Height: 6'0"
>Weight: 175
>Address: Whispering Sands Apartments,
>300 Sandhill Road. Apt # 15, Page, Arizona 86040
>Property Type: Rental
>Rent amount: $575 / month
>Driver's License State: Arizona
>Title: Information Technology Support Specialist
>Annual Income: $62,000.00
>Years at H&S: 5
>Marital Status: Divorced
>Children: 1 (daughter)

> Criminal record: None
> Social Media: Twitter

JASON HAS DONE a good job avoiding the IT department. They'd be able to pick up on his skillset, and we want to keep that on the down low. As far as they're concerned, we're auditors in search of the missing money. What they don't know is Jason's hacked into the systems multiple times, searching for IP addresses and other trails that could lead us to others in the company.

I know whoever did this could be anyone, but there are personality traits that carry through to most embezzlers. Like the fact they're usually older than other criminals, over thirty, because they begin their criminal activity at a much later age. Most are married with traditional family situations. As a rule, they have higher levels of education than the average criminal. The majority of perpetrators are white. Nearly all of them are first-time offenders with clean employment histories. The majority of offenders used to be men but since more women are in leadership roles, those numbers have increased, which is why some refer to it as a "pink-collar crime." I just call it a crime. Period.

I hear Agatha's breathing even out, which tells me she's asleep. Her soft body is pressed against mine, and it's nice. No, that's not right. It's better than nice. It's fucking amazing. Catherine was a beautiful woman but nothing about her was soft. She worked out more than I did, and I think she could probably bench press me. I'm not criticizing. It was part of our job to keep our bodies in shape. They're as much a weapon as a gun sometimes. But now, with this beautiful, curvy woman in my arms, I now know what's been missing in my life. Pulling her in more tightly, I close my eyes and listen to the rhythm of her little snores. I let my body relax, because for the first time in my life, I know this is it. Home.

～

I STARE as Agatha smears cream cheese on her bagel. "So, how do you like the bagels?" I woke up with the sun out of habit, so I decided to run out and get my girl her bagels. When I returned, she was still asleep. I brewed some coffee, checked my messages, sent a few, and was contemplating showering when sleeping beauty finally woke up.

Biting into her breakfast, she speaks with her mouth full, "Good. Fanks."

I chuckle as I prepare my bagel. I waited to let her choose her favorite flavor, cinnamon crunch. Note to self, get two of those next time.

I select a cinnamon raisin bagel and swipe a thin layer of cream cheese over the top. Before I take a bite, I ask her, "So, tell me about Miriam Smith." Agatha's take on my short list of suspects is helpful, but I do know a little about Miriam from my background check.

Miriam Smith
    Age: 56
    DOB: 7-10-62
    Height: 5'8"
    Weight: 265
    Address: 15 Reflection Canyon, Page, Arizona 86040
    Property Type: Rent
    Payment amount: $2094 / month
    Driver's License State: Arizona

> Title: Human Resources Director
> Annual Income: $85,210.00
> Years at H&S: 5.5
> Marital Status: Divorced
> Children: 1 (daughter)
> Criminal record: None
> Social Media: Facebook

"Well, I don't really know her very well," she says, sipping her coffee. "I talked to her during my performance reviews and whenever I was turned down for a promotion." She rolls her eyes as she takes another bite.

"How often did that happen?"

"Too often." Wiping a little cream cheese from her lips, she adds, "Three times since I got my CPA."

"Why?"

She shrugs, "Hell if I know. They always chose someone below me. Usually a man and someone *I* trained. Miriam always hinted that it was Drake's decision. She seemed to feel bad about it, but..." She shrugs again. "What're you gonna do?"

"Sue."

"Really? Wouldn't that have made things awkward at work?" She laughs, but there's no humor in it.

"Is there anything else about Miriam that stands out? Something about her that doesn't make sense?"

She stops eating and looks at me. "Well..."

I move closer to her. I know she's going to give me something good.

"She never *knew* anything."

"Meaning?"

"About Human Resources. She never knew the answer. Whenever I asked her something about a company policy, insurance, or even about advancement training, she never knew the answer."

"I can see why that'd be something that would stand out."

"Yeah, even general staff training she pushed off on Trent. He used to complain about the fact that all she did was sit in her office and play games on her phone."

"So, she's lazy?"

"That's not what I'm talking about, but, yeah, she's probably lazy too. I just don't think she knows anything about Human Resources. She used to tell me and Camille that she'd have to get back to us whenever we asked her something, pretending she was busy doing something more important."

Agatha takes a very aggressive bite out of her bagel. Not waiting to chew and swallow, she adds, "It's booship. See sood know it." Her brows are furrowed into the most adorable frown. I want to kiss those crinkled lines on her forehead but I'd better not.

To clarify, I repeat what I think she said, "It's bullshit? She should know it?"

"Myeah."

"She *should* know it. You're right." Ah, hell, I do it. I kiss her on her frown lines. "I'll do some more digging on Miriam. You ready to talk about Drake?"

The scowl on her face intensifies. "Om eating." She chews. "Gib me a thec."

"Right. Give you a sec."

"Myeah."

So, I do. We both finish our bagels. I want another one, but I'll wait until she's finished giving me her thoughts on Drake. My gut tells me they aren't going to be kind.

CHAPTER TWENTY-FOUR

AGATHA

I NEED to get out of my house. I feel like a cloistered nun, hidden away from life for going on three weeks now. "You want to get out of here for a while?"

Ian's sitting on one of my barstools in only his jeans and Harry Potter tee. *Sigh.* I could get used to this.

"What'd you have in mind?"

"Have you been out to Lake Powell yet? If not, we could take a ride out there. It's really beautiful." What am I doing? I just asked him out. *Gah, bad idea.*

"Sure. We could have a picnic."

OMG! A picnic? Yes! *Be cool, Aggie. Be cool.* Shrugging, I say, "Sure. Sounds fun." *More than fun. It sounds amazing.* "Do you like egg salad? Because I make a mean egg salad."

Ian approaches from behind. I feel his body against my back and his arm wrap around me. When his lips touch my neck, I tilt my head to give him room for more.

"I love egg salad." He nibbles on my earlobe, and my nipples harden. "And I really love that you want to make it for me."

"Didn't Catherine ever cook?" Shit, why did I ever mention Catherine's name? I feel his body shaking. Oh no! I've upset him. I turn quickly, ready to apologize. "Ian I'm...." Wait. He's laughing? "You're laughing?"

"Yeah. That was funny shit. Did Catherine cook?" He kisses me between the eyes for the second time today. "Definitely not. She could barely microwave popcorn."

"Oh."

"Yeah. Oh. So, anything you feel like cooking, I'll eat with a grin on my face, because I'll appreciate it more than you'll ever know, honey." This time he kisses me lower, right smack dab on my lips.

It's a quick kiss. I wish it was slow.

"HOLY SHIT, AGATHA. THIS IS AMAZING," Ian says, breathless.

I love Ian's reaction to Lake Powell. It is one of those places everyone should see. It's breathtaking, especially from our perch way above the lake. We used to come here a lot when we were kids. When Mom first got sick, Dad would bring her here, just the two of them sometimes. It's peaceful and exhilarating at the same time. It's actually a reservoir that has carved a serpentine space around two peaks. Striations in the rock show its history— and the hundreds, maybe millions of years it took to create it.

"You like it, then?" Who wouldn't like it? I just want to be sure.

"I had no idea there was a place like this here, honey." Ian raises his arm, resting it around my shoulder, pulling me into him. I lay my head on his shoulder. We stand there just like that for a good long while.

I think I get why this was Mom and Dad's favorite place. It just might be mine now too.

CHAPTER TWENTY-FIVE

Ian

I'VE JUST FINISHED my second egg salad sandwich, and I'm wishing for a third.

"Here," Agatha says, holding out half of hers.

"No. That's yours. You eat it." I'm serious. She should eat it.

"You have no idea how happy I am you like my food. Eat it. I'll fill up on chips and my apple."

"You sure?"

"Positive."

God, I love this woman. I freeze. I didn't mean that. Really. I didn't. "Thanks, Agatha." Ignoring my stupid internal thoughts, I stuff my face. Time to eat my feelings. Problem solved.

After the food's gone, we clean up our trash and then settle back onto the blanket Agatha packed for us. "So. Tell me about Drake."

"Ugh. No," she whines. "I was having fun."

I roll onto my side to look at her. Her hair is down and it's fluttering around in a slight breeze. It looks shiny and soft. I know from personal experience that it's as silky as it looks. Next, I take in her clothes. She's wearing a plain navy tee with short sleeves and a V-neck that gives me a glimpse of the tops of her full breasts. She's paired the shirt with denim cutoffs. I've been doing my goddamn best to keep my eyes above her waist, when all I want to do is pull her down so I can slide those little shorts right down her sexy-as-fuck legs. Forcing my eyes up, I see pink cheeks from the sun—or maybe they're pink from thinking of the other fun things we could do. "Oh, yeah? So, what do you want to do instead?" My dick is hoping she wants some naughty fun.

"Anything but talk about Drake Gargoyle."

"Anything?" I don't give her a chance to overthink. I reach out, wrap my arm around her outstretched legs, and pull her down next to me. "Oh, Agatha Palmer." I kiss her on the corner of her mouth. She tastes like apple.

"What?"

"Nothing behind me..." I kiss her lips. "Everything ahead of me..." I kiss her furrowed brow, then her lips again.

In a soft, emotional voice, she asks, "D-Did you just quote Jack Kerouac while we o-overlook Lake Powell?"

Oh shit, she's starting to cry? What the fuck did I say? "Agatha?"

Shaking her head, she smiles as she wipes away the wetness. "No." She grasps my hand. "This was one of my mom's favorite places, and you just quoted her favorite book."

"I'm sorry. I didn't mean to make you sad."

"No. You misunderstand. What you just said... I'll never forget it. I'll never forget this day. I'll never forget *you*, Ian Burke."

"Jesus, Agatha." I sit up, then pull myself up to standing, taking a few steps away from our picnic. When I turn to say what I need to say, she's gone. I look toward my car and see her racing away in that direction. Fuck. "Agatha!" I shout.

I know she can hear me but she's ignoring me. Go figure.

"Agatha!" I yell again as I run for her. "Goddammit, woman. Stop!"

CHAPTER TWENTY-SIX

AGATHA

STUPID, stupid Agatha. You had to open your stupid mouth just then. I always make everything so awkward. *So freaking awkward.*

"Agatha!"

Ignore him. He's going to smooth things over, but I'll still feel like the biggest idiot that ever lived.

"Agatha!"

Keep walking.

"Goddammit, woman. Stop!"

I stop. Because I have to. I'm at the car, and he's got the keys. "Shit." I set the blanket down. The one I whipped off the ground so fast, my picnic basket took a tumble. No worries. I can get another antique wicker basket like the one my grandmother used to use at every single Palmer family reunion since the beginning of time.

I look to my left, then my right. There's no escape. Maybe if

I start walking, someone will be nice enough to pick me up. Oh, shit. What if the nice person ended up being a serial killer? I can see it now on the nightly news: *Agatha Palmer, embezzler, was picked up by the Lake Powell Perpetrator. Her body was never found.*

"Goddammit, Agatha." Ian is panting behind me. "Before you run off down the road, I need for you to hear what I was going to say back there."

I know he's pointing back to the picnic site. *I hope my basket is still there.*

"Would you please look at me?"

Oh, he sounds so sad. Serious, but sad. Reluctantly, I turn.

"I was going to say that I hated to hear you talk about me like I'm already gone."

"I—"

He presses his finger over my lips. "Let me finish, please."

"Okay."

"I like you."

Eye roll.

"Don't roll your pretty eyes at me, Agatha." He chuckles. "I'll never forget today either. Or last night, or this morning, or the night before that, or the night we fell asleep on the couch, or the lasagna we ate together sitting at your little counter. I won't forget the night you wore that ugly wig and I still thought you were the most beautiful girl I'd ever seen, and I definitely won't ever forget the day we met, when you looked into my eyes with your pretty gray ones and told me you were innocent. That's all it took, honey. I was fucking hooked right there on the street. I believed you, and I knew right then and there that you were wronged, and that's the moment I made it my mission to find the *real* thief."

I feel tears slide down my cheeks.

He stares at me. "Shit, honey. Don't cry again. I can't take it when you cry."

"Happy tears, Ian. Happy tears."

"They're tears. They're all bad."

I shake my head as I wrap my arms around his neck and press my cheek into his tee. "No, not all tears are bad. Some are happy, some are cathartic, some just pop up out of nowhere for no good reason."

He continues his speech. "I don't want you to put an expiration date on us. It's too soon to determine what this is between us, but I want the time to do that. Do you?"

I nod, because I'm really crying now. "I do."

I feel him release a deep breath and hear him say, "Thank fuck."

Ian

"YOU WANT to know what I think of Drake?" Agatha asks with an arched brow.

We're driving back from Lake Powell after a long talk and a short make-out session. We have to get back because Agatha's got another catering gig tonight.

"Yeah. I'd *finally* like to hear your keen observations."

Ignoring my little jab, she states, "Okay. Drake is a jerk."

"I know. I hate working for the guy. He's a tool."

"I know." She groans. "Pretty please, can we not talk about him?"

I'll give her a pass for a little while. "So, where is this job tonight?"

"I shouldn't tell you, but you'll probably just follow me anyway." She laughs. "It's in north Flagstaff."

"Again?"

"Yes, but Beth, the owner, said that this one is only about

fifty people and it's at some sort of club. It's not supposed to run late."

"Ah, I see. So, I'll drive you down and wait for you."

"No. You won't. Go home. Get some rest. I'll call you when I get home."

I shake my head. She's not going to give in on this.

"I promise you. If you want to try to make this thing work," she points to both of us, "you need to know I'm independent. You can't just follow me around because you're a big, bad secret agent."

"Uh-huh."

"You're going to follow me anyway, aren't you?"

"Yep." This is no time to let our guard down.

"Fine. Let's save gas. You can drive me."

"Great. Let's grab something to eat on the way to Flagstaff."

I hear her hum in agreement, but she says nothing.

"Agatha, I don't have to drive you down."

"You'll just follow me."

This was true. I will follow her. "True."

WHILE AGATHA SHOWERED AND CHANGED, I washed up our picnic dishes. After that, I drove us to my hotel so I could clean up and change too. I've been staying in a one-bedroom suite in the nicest hotel in Page. Not that there were many to choose from, since Page is relatively small. If it weren't for Heart & Sole Shoes being headquartered here, there would be no hotels available at all.

The main part of the suite is outfitted with a small kitchenette and a living room with a sofa, chair, coffee table, and flat-screen television mounted to the wall. The one and only window in the space looks out over the parking lot, but now that

I've been there, I can see the rocks that lead to Lake Powell in the distance, so the view isn't horrible.

I left Agatha sitting on my sofa while I headed into the bathroom, stripped down, turned on the shower, and stepped inside. I was doing my best to hurry but I kept picturing Agatha in her pencil skirt, white blouse, and flat shoes. Back at her place, she stepped out of her room wearing black slacks instead of the skirt, and I made some kind of noise.

"What?" she asked.

"Nothing."

"No, tell me." She looked worried.

"I like you in the skirt."

"You do?" I think she was sincerely surprised by the comment.

"I do. You've got great legs, honey."

"I do?"

I chuckled and stepped toward her. "You're a sexy woman, Agatha."

"I am?"

I laughed again, swatting her bottom. "We need to get going."

"Let me change first." She raced back into her bedroom, but she was back out in minutes wearing the tight pencil skirt. "Better?"

I looked at her from top to bottom, stopping for an extra moment on her legs. "Oh, yeah."

Her face blushed to a pretty shade of pink. I'd have loved to take a moment to investigate that blush, but if we wanted to get food before work, we had to get moving.

Stepping out of the shower, I realize I forgot to grab clothes. Wrapping a towel around my waist, I open the door and step into my adjoining bedroom. As I'm about to walk to my dresser, I catch a glimpse of black and white on my bed. Agatha.

"Hey," I say, a tad surprised. She's leaning back, sitting on the edge of my bed, legs crossed, feet bare. I want to ask her what she's doing but I already know. I quickly glance at the clock on the nightstand then back at her. "We'll never have time to get dinner."

"We can get something after."

"True. Very true." I reach her in two long strides, sliding my hand behind her head and kissing the fuck out of her. "This what you want?" I ask as I let my lips kiss down the column of her neck.

"Yes," she says as I bite her earlobe.

"You sure?"

"Ian..."

I don't need her to say any more. As fast as I can, I work to unbutton the white blouse, careful not to rip it open like I want to. Her hands fumble along with mine, working the buttons free. Once it's open, I pull the blouse down over her shoulders, letting her work it off her wrists. That's good, because I've got other things on my mind. Her tits. She doesn't have huge breasts, but what she does have is overflowing from her basic white bra. So much so that I can lean down and lick the top of one globe, then the other. "Fuck, honey." The towel around my waist isn't going to last much longer. My dick is fighting for escape. "I want you so bad."

CHAPTER TWENTY-EIGHT

AGATHA

IAN'S HAND is running over the tops of my breasts almost reverently. That is, until he suddenly grasps one bra cup, pulling it down far enough for my nipple to appear. "Beautiful," he says softly right before he latches on, sucking hard.

"Oh, God, Ian." It's such a shocking sensation that I arch my back off the bed.

His hands roam down my sides to the bottom edge of my skirt, sliding beneath the edge. I feel the warmth of his palm as he skims up my outer, then inner thigh.

"You sure, Agatha?" His voice is like warm honey, smooth and delicious.

I nod.

"I need your words, sweetheart."

"Yes. I'm sure."

His fingers slide out from beneath my skirt to wrap around

my waist, fumbling with the button. Once he gets it, he slides the zipper down. Patting my bottom, he growls, "Off."

I raise my hips off the bed to assist in easing the skirt down.

"Wiggle, honey."

I wiggle my ass back and forth as he pushes down my skirt, leaving me in only my white cotton bikini panties that match my equally un-sexy white cotton bra. In seconds, the bra is gone too. Replacing it? Ian's warm hands. He's cupping both breasts, and I love it. I feel myself grow wet from just his fingers swiping over my nipples. Nipples that are hard and erect. "Ian," I whisper.

"I want you so much, honey."

I want him too.

His hands begin to knead my breasts, and every once in a while, his fingers pinch and pluck on my nipples, like he's playing an instrument. It's turning me on so much. Reaching out toward his towel, I can feel him, long and hard. "Ian?"

"Yeah?" His voice is husky and deep.

"You've got too many clothes on."

I think that's the cue he needed. Chuckling, he steps back. I take a moment to gawk at the man's upper body. He's muscled for sure, but he's lean too. There are indentations showing me where his abdominals are but he's no gym rat. When he lets the towel drop to the floor, I look lower at a completely nude, amazingly hard and erect Ian Burke. The man is beautiful. There are no other words for it. His penis is big. Not porn star big, but bigger than I've ever seen. Or felt.

He has to know I'm staring at it, because he moves his hand to it and begins to rub up and down the shaft. "Take your panties off, babe."

Ooh, he broke out the "babe." This is getting serious. And fun. "Make me."

He smirks, or at least I think he does, since I'm still staring, like a pervert, at his dick. "Is it going to be like that? You going to be a naughty girl?"

Oh, shit. I just came.

"Uh-huh," I say, all Marilyn Monroe-like.

"Babe."

I finally look up at his face. I had to tear my eyes away from *it* just as it started to leak. "Yeah?"

"Lie back."

I move up onto the bed, placing my head on a pillow, I watch him place one knee on the edge. "I hope to play that game with you sometime when we've got more time, but tonight I just want to be inside you."

"Oh." *I'm for that.*

He slides his fingers into the edge of my underwear, and his short fingernails drag against my skin as they move down over my center. When he pulls the panel away from me, seeing me down there, he growls, "Beautiful. So pretty, honey."

Yay! He likes my hoo-ha. Don't get me wrong, I didn't think *down there* was going to scare him or anything, since I keep myself lady-scaped. Keely is a big proponent of Brazilians for all of her sisters, but I can't go there. I can shave myself, *thankyou- verymuch.* I do *not* need the skin of my privates peeled off by hot wax and a stranger.

When his hand slides further into my undies, I refocus my attention on him. God, it feels good. His hands are magic. He knows just where to touch me, and how to use his fingers. For example, when he circles them around my clit and then deep inside, it makes me open my legs wider to encourage him. "Feels so good."

"Are you achy for me, Agatha?"

God, yes. "So achy, Ian."

It happens so fast. One minute I'm on my back, legs wide open, his hands in all the right places. The next minute, my panties are flying through the air and Ian's on his back and my, err, center is above his face. "Lower yourself down. Hold on to the headboard, Agatha."

"I've never...."

"No one's ever tasted you?"

I can't speak. I shake my head, because no one has ever gone down on me. "Oh, my God." His tongue. Hell, his entire mouth is over me. I feel his lips down there. It's like a kiss, only better. *Waaayyy* better. His tongue slides up and down through my crease, stopping at my clit on each pass, paying special attention to the little pack of nerves. He licks. He sucks, and I swear, he nibbles. "Oh, my God."

His palms slide up behind me onto my ass, squeezing and pulling me down at the same time. I'm stiffening up. I don't want to kill the man. I'm no skinny-mini.

"Get out of your head, Agatha. You look beautiful from here. Let me." He sucks on my clit, and I squeak.

Growling into me, he repeats, "Just relax, honey. Let me do this."

I nod frantically. "Do it." *Please.*

His hands are magic, but his tongue and mouth are intergalactic. I feel the orgasm start in my belly. I clench around his fingers that are now moving in and out of me. The combination of his mouth and fingers is pushing me higher. The tingles start, and I release a low, guttural moan. I feel myself pulsing and vibrating around his fingers. In my entire adult life, I've never come that hard. Ever.

In a daze, I feel his hands nudge me backwards until I'm straddling his waist. His face is shining with my, uh, my essence. I lean down and kiss his lips gently. He takes it further, bringing his hand behind my head to pull me closer. We kiss, and I taste myself. I have no idea who I've become, because I like it. I deepen the kiss, sweeping my tongue into his mouth. I want him. Inside.

When I'm directly over him, he looks into my eyes. "Are you on birth control, Agatha?"

I nod. "The pill."

"Do you trust me when I tell you I'm clean? I've only ever gone without with my ex-wife, and that was a long time ago."

"I trust you," I whisper. I wish he hadn't brought her up, but it had to be said, I guess. "I'm clean, I've never done it without a condom either." Not that I've done it enough to worry about, but once is enough, I guess.

"Okay. You ready for me?" he asks as he presses me down until I feel him at my entrance.

"I'm ready."

His palms press down on my waist at the same time I lower myself onto him. We moan in unison. It's a tight fit, made tighter by the orgasm I just had. It feels like it takes me forever to get fully seated, but once I do, I lean forward, running my palms over his chest. I just want to stay right here forever. God, he's deep. So damn deep. "Ian. Oh, wow."

With a grunt and clenched teeth, he mutters, "Come on, fuck me, Agatha."

I lift myself up using his chest for balance. Up until he says, "Fuck. So sweet. So wet." It's hot that he's only using one- or two-word phrases.

When he grips my waist, plunging up into me, it's my turn to speak cavewoman. "Don't stop, Ian." I want to move too but he's holding me steady, thrusting, pounding in and out. In and out. I've never been on top before. If I'd known it was going to be like this, I'd have tried it once or twice, or a million times.

Swiping at his hands, I urge him to let go so I can move on my own. Placing my hands behind him, gripping the top of the headboard, I lift up when he's down and press down when he moves up. In no time, we've got a rhythm that's fast and so, so good. He wraps his arms around me, pulling my chest down. Taking one of my hard peaks into his mouth, he sucks on it. I feel him running a finger over and around my clit, all while we're still moving. The man is talented. I'm in sensation overload. Throwing my head back, I orgasm so hard it makes my body tremble.

Ian picks up the pace, his thrusts growing more and more frantic. Pressing in one last, hard time, he releases a growl. A sound that could rival mine.

Panting, he wraps his arms around me, pulling me down until we're chest to chest. "Jesus, Agatha," he whispers, kissing my shoulder, then my neck, my chin, and up to my lips. "That was..."

"Yeah." My body is a rubbery blob. I can barely move, let alone speak more than one word, but I try. "It was..."

"Everything," he says sweetly.

I blink, taking in his word choice. Looking into his eyes, all I see is sincerity. So, I say the only thing that feels right. "Yeah."

"SO, WHAT'RE YOU HUNGRY FOR?" I say, looking over at Ian. When he gives me a sexy smirk, I roll my eyes. "Later. I'm starving. I had to work three hours with a growling stomach since we didn't have time to eat before work."

"Whose fault is that?" he says with a chuckle.

"Yours."

"Ah, I see. That's how you want to play it?" He reaches out, squeezing my thigh.

"Nah. It's both of our faults." I hesitate, adding, "It was worth it, right?"

He turns to look at me, and his eyes have grown soft, as does his smile. "Well worth it." I watch as Ian pulls into a restaurant I've never heard of. "This place is great. Lots of variety, so you can pick something that sounds good to you."

"I'm ravenous. I could eat anything."

When I get his sexy look again, I giggle. "Later."

"Promise?"

Giving him my own sexy look back, I start to open my car door just as I spot Camille exiting the restaurant. "Hey, there's Camille," I say excitedly. "I haven't talked to her in forever."

As I'm about to push open the door and yell for her, Ian grasps my arm. "Shush. Shut the door."

"Why?"

"The light," he says, pointing up to the inside dome light.

I quickly shut my door just as two other people exit the restaurant. Two people I recognize. "What are *they* doing here?" I look over at Ian. "Why are they with Camille?"

We stare in silence as all three get into the same vehicle.

"I don't know, but we're going to find out."

I rebuckle my seat belt as Ian eases out of our parking spot.

"Keep your eye on the vehicle. We'll need to stay back a few cars."

"We're following them?"

"Yep."

If I wasn't completely confused about what I just saw, I'd be excited I was playing detective with Ian right now. But I am, so I'm not.

We follow them south all the way through Flagstaff until Ian mumbles, "Wow, Mountainaire."

"What about it?"

"It's posh. A very exclusive suburb of Flagstaff."

Posh? Did he just say posh? I want to laugh but all of this is freaking me out. Why would Camille get into the car with *them?* I'm afraid to ask what he thinks. My gut tells me this isn't a good sign for me and my bestie. Unless... "Do you think they kidnapped her?"

Giving me the side-eye again, Ian shakes his head. "No."

No? That's it? "You have a theory then?"

"I don't. Not yet. I'm working on it." He reaches out and squeezes my knee. "But what I do know is that I'm about to make your dreams come true."

"We're not having sex in the car, Ian." Okay, *maybe* we could have sex in the car.

Chuckling, he leans over the center console to kiss my cheek. "No, a different dream of yours."

I wait. I want to hear what dream he thinks he's going to fulfill.

"We're going on a stakeout."

I watch as the car Camille's in pulls into a long driveway that leads to a huge house. "We are?" I say excitedly. "Now?" *OMG, I've always wanted to do a stakeout.*

"Now."

"Oh, shit, Ian. I wish we'd gotten some food. I'm starving."

Reaching behind him, Ian grasps a white, plastic grocery bag. "I've got snacks."

I peek inside and see a plethora of treats. Some sweet, some salty. Leaning over to the glove box, he pops it open, retrieving a bottle of water. "You come prepared."

"I do."

"So, how long do we need to sit here?"

"As long as it takes."

As long as it takes. There's a life lesson in there somewhere, but right now, I'm too hungry to figure it out. Stuffing my face with the first thing I grab, I nod. "M'okay."

CHAPTER TWENTY-NINE

Ian

One week later

"THANK you all for taking time out of your busy day to meet with me." I look around the room at Drake, Kim, Miriam, Trent, and Monica. I've asked them all to meet me in conference room three, where it all began.

"What's this about? Did you find the money? Did you get that bitch to tell you where she hid it?" spits Drake.

"Cutting right to the chase, Drake. I like that." I stand up from my chair so that I'm looking down at all of them. It's a psychological play, one I've used before. "First, let me tell you that this case has been particularly complicated." I turn toward the floor-to-ceiling windows. "One that's had its twists and turns." I'm prolonging this, attempting to see how impatient they become. One person in particular.

"Drake? Is this really necessary?"

Bingo.

Turning to face them, I state matter-of-factly, "Let me cut to the chase. Agatha Palmer didn't take that money."

Drake snorts, while the others look shocked. "You're fucking her. Of course you'd say that."

Jesus, Drake is crass. That's extremely inappropriate. Ignoring it for the time being, I add, "Here's what we know." I tell them what we discovered, well, most of what we discovered. That whoever took the money controlled Agatha's computer remotely and only paid the invoices in question when she was away from her desk. I tell them about the nanny cam and about the obvious use. of names any idiot would find if they were looking for it.

"She wasn't very bright. What do you expect?" mutters Miriam.

Kim looks surprised, which gives me pause. "You don't agree, Kim?"

"No. Agatha is whip-smart."

Drake scoffs again. "That's not what I heard. I heard she barely passed her CPA exam. The rumor is that she cheated."

Leaning forward in her seat, Kim turns to Drake, but he's not looking back. "Drake, she scored a ninety-eight."

Drake's head slowly rotates toward Kim. "A ninety-eight?"

"Out of ninety-nine. And she didn't cheat. I was with her."

"You took your exam at the same time?" This time it's Monica asking.

"Yes. And in case you were curious, I got an eighty-one."

"Well, you've got to be mistaken," Drake blusters. "I have it on good authority—"

"Who's good authority?" I ask, already knowing the answer.

"I'd rather not say," he says gruffly.

"No matter. That little tidbit of information only hurts your theory. She was trying to outsmart us by using those silly business names." Miriam has decided to jump in feet first—to put in her two cents.

Ignoring her, I look at Drake. "May I continue?" No one attempts to stop me, so I say, "We found the remote access coding on Miss Palmer's computer. We searched servers and the cloud for any activity that would link the other party involved, but to no avail."

"See?" Drake again. "It's her. It's Palmer."

Is he even listening? Ignoring him, I continue. "We determined that whoever did it most likely used a cell phone. That's why I've put a call in to a buddy of mine at the Bureau to get access to the cell phone records of any person or persons who would have means, motive, and opportunity to steal from H&S."

"How many people are on *that* list?" asks Trent.

"I'm not at liberty to say. What I do know is we've narrowed down the pool significantly."

"How long will that take? They're breathing down my neck about this shit." Drake's face has gotten red, and sweat is starting to drip down his forehead.

"As soon as he gets back to me, I'll be able to give you a timeline, but I'm comfortable saying two days, three at the most."

"Holy fuck. Why does this shit take so long?" Drake is visibly panting. He doesn't look well, especially now that he's clutching his chest.

"Drake? Honey?" Monica rushes to Drake's side.

Honey? She called him honey? That's just great. Jesus, are they sleeping together? If so, they sure as hell did a good job keeping *that* under wraps. I look over at Kim again, who's staring back at me knowingly. She gives me a slight nod. I guess it wasn't as under wraps as I thought. It explains the fancy shoes and clothes. Gifts, most likely, from Drake to Monica. God, I fucking hate cheaters.

"I'm fine, Mon. This whole thing is just stressful."

"I know, baby." Her hand is on his head. She's petting him. "Let Ian finish what he's got to say, then we'll let you have a lie-down. Mm-kay?"

"Okay," he whimpers, sounding like a little boy.

Monica turns to me, never taking her hands off her boss. "So, we'll know something in a few days."

"I'll see if I can expedite this. Three days tops. Let me add that we should also be able to track the other accounts from that same phone. We suspect they did everything from the one device. Cleaner that way. Less chance of screwups."

"Fine. Go. Do it. I want to know the second you know anything," snaps Drake.

"I will. Before I go, does anyone have any other questions?"

Trent raises his hand like he's in high school. "Are any of them in this room?" asks Trent again.

"The suspects? I can't say."

"Can't you give us a hint?" Trent is starting to annoy the fuck out of me.

However, it does help lead me to something I was hoping I could say. "I can't give you a name, but I will tell you that my lead suspect is someone close to Agatha."

"Close to her?" asks Kim. "Logistically or emotionally?"

Excellent. That was exactly the kind of question I was hoping for. "Both."

"No way," whispers Trent.

Now they know I'm talking about Camille. They have to. The trap has been set. Now, let's see how the head rat reacts to that.

CHAPTER THIRTY

IT TOOK us a week to get our ducks in a row. Enough time for Ian to find the needed evidence, attempt to locate the money, and plan the sting operation. Ooh, I love the sound of that: *sting operation.* I get shivers from just saying it. In order to accomplish all that, he first had to go over Drake's head to the H&S CEO, Brad Mills, since he believed strongly that Drake wouldn't be impartial or rational. The other reason was so he could get law enforcement involved and that had to be approved by Brad.

I've been working right alongside Ian in this process. Since my expertise is in accounting, I have been acting as a forensic accountant to help in the search for the rest of the money. Unfortunately, we found a trail but no accounts. According to Ian's friend with the Bureau, that most likely means the money is offshore, out of the country. If that's the case, that would bring the FBI into the fold. Apparently, the US government doesn't like it when you hide money in other countries. Go figure.

I can't lie. Working on the investigation has been exhilarating. Not just working side by side with Ian, because that has been amazingly fun (and sexy at times), but with Jason, a tech guy named Basil, and Brad, the company CEO. Fun fact: Mr. Mills had no idea I'd been fired. I'm not sure if that lack of knowledge was his fault or Drake's. If I had to guess, though, based on the expression on Brad Mills's face when he heard the entire story, I'd say Drake kept him in the dark about the majority of the embezzlement information. I'd also bet Drake's days at H&S are numbered. But who knows? Corporate America doesn't always play like the rest of us. Only time will tell.

So, with Brad's okay, we've worked in the offices at night since we didn't want to tip any of the suspects off of our dastardly plot. We used that time to install our own nanny cams *with* audio in each of the appropriate offices as well as apps and devices to monitor emails, telephone calls, and texts. The process has been fascinating. Even now, when I'm merely sitting in the temporary control room of Phoenix Cyber Security on the thirteenth floor of H&S watching the monitors, I'm vibrating with excitement and have been since five this morning. Ian snuck me in early so no one would know I was on the property and I could watch this all unfold.

Ian hasn't yet returned from his meeting in conference room three with the original members of my firing squad. Ha! Get it? Firing squad.

"I got it," mutters Jason.

Oops. I guess I said that aloud.

"Here he comes." I stare at one of the monitors as Ian steps out of the conference room. I watch as his eyes move up to the camera. I know he's looking at me because he winks.

"He looks pleased as punch," says Jason.

We watched his meeting thanks to our surveillance cameras, and I have to say, Ian Burke is brilliant. And sexy. So damn sexy.

"He does look pleased." As he should. I know the basic plan, but now that we're all here, waiting, I'm worried it's not going to work.

Ian enters the room, shutting the door behind him quickly. Pressing the lock down, he walks over to me, wraps his arms around me, and kisses me. "It was better than I'd hoped. Now that they know we're about to nail them, the rats will scurry around trying to cover their tracks like they're on a sinking ship."

"Little do they know you already got those phone records." I giggle because I'm nervous and because Ian is so hot when he's being all private dickish.

Wait. Um. You know what I mean, right?

"We do. And since we know there are three involved—"

"There are always three involved," interjects Jason. "At least, that's what I read."

Ignoring him, I repeat, "We know the three involved plus we've got the Feds in on this. Their phones are tapped, computers are monitored, and their offices wired. I don't think it'll take them long to make a move."

We stare at the monitors, one of which is focused on Camille's cubicle. My heart hurts over everything I've learned about her since last week. I've discovered her real name us Katelyn Camille Bartlett. I know she was hired by Miriam, her mother, about a month after Miriam started working here. Miriam also hired her husband and Camille's father, Victor Smiley, around that same time. I also know they've done this before, under different names, of course, at the last three places they've worked. Each time, they've framed someone who didn't deserve to be framed and they've stolen several million dollars along the way. It's how they can afford the fancy house in Mountainaire, I guess.

"I still don't get how they got away with the fake names," asked Jason one late night. "And what about taxes and shit?"

I answered, since taxes are an area I understand. "Since Miriam was the Human Resources Director of a very small department, and Trent was only in charge of much of the hiring, she took on the payroll, which meant she not only had untethered access to those records, she submitted everything to the IRS, so she could use their real names there but use the false name for the H&S internal records. No one but her knew their real names. If that had been flagged by the Feds, they'd contact her about it so she could explain it away."

"She could cover all three of their asses from her perch as head of HR," adds Ian.

"Wow, smart," Jason says with awe. "Fucked-up, but smart."

He was right about that.

Ian really did call a buddy of his at the Bureau to call in a favor. His friend ran the social security numbers of the three in question. From there, they did a deeper search, discovering their familial relationship. The three used aliases but they always seemed to be a variation of their real names. For example, Bartlett was Miriam's maiden name, and Miriam was married once before to a guy named Dave Smith. Victor's first name is James, so he's gone by Victor Smiley, James Smiley, as well as James Victor. Clever. Right?

Nah. They're terrible people. They don't deserve to be called clever. That's too nice.

Reaching back, I grab Ian's hand. "There she goes."

We all lean forward as Miriam leaves her office, making a beeline for the stairwell. Once inside, we turn our focus to another monitor. As soon as she pulls out her cell phone, Jason unmutes the sound in the stairwell.

"You recording this?" Ian asks Jason.

"Hell, yeah. In HD."

Awesome.

"Katie. Shut up and listen to me right now. You need to ditch the phone," hisses Miriam into her cell phone.

We watch Miriam as she appears to be listening to her daughter.

"Don't question me, you little shit. Go on break, walk down the street, and toss that thing in the river." She pauses. "I know there's no river close by; just stomp on it and chuck in the trash." She's about to hang up when she adds, "And pull the fucking SIM card out and break it the fuck up." She's listening again. "Jesus fucking Christ. For once in your goddamn life, listen to me. Do. It. Now."

She pauses again.

"Well, I don't know. Alls I know to do is destroy the phone. You and your stupid dad are the tech geniuses." Then she mutters, "Some fucking tech geniuses. We're going to get caught if you don't do what I say. We need to get gone before they figure it out about me and Vic. They're already on to you, Katie. Now do as I fucking say."

She presses the end call button, and then dials another number.

"Vic. They know. That cocksucker Ian figured it out."

Jason snickers, and I giggle.

"He's going to get the Feds in on this. We need to destroy everything. Move the money." Pausing again, she whines, "Why the fuck don't you two ever listen to me? Move. The. Fucking. Money." Her voice is now at shouting level. "Now! And don't use your damn phone. They're trying to get cell phone records. Use your computer."

"Yes," Ian says excitedly. It's what we need to locate the cash. We're recording keystrokes on all three of their desktop computers so if he uses his, we'll be able to track every single digit.

Miriam hangs up, leans against the wall, rests her head back, and looks up.

"Smile. You're on Jason's camera," Jason sings.

Miriam must have seen the camera, because her eyes have grown round and a tad buggy. She holds up her phone but thinks better of it. Instead, she scurries out of the stairwell.

I giggle again, because nerves, and because this is so frigging exciting. "This is the most fun I've ever had. God, I want to be a private dick."

"You don't have the equipment, darlin'," chuckles Jason.

"Shut up, asswipe. She means private detective."

Ignoring Ian's dig, Jason coos, "Come work with us. You'd be a pretty addition to the crew."

"No," I mutter. "You didn't just say that." Jason sure can be creepy.

"He did," says Ian, watching the monitors.

"What?" Jason asks, confused.

"You're too young to be such a sexist idiot, Jason."

"I'm not sexist. I love women."

I groan loudly. "You need to take a class or something." I turn to Ian. "Can you make him take a class?"

"I'll get on that, honey."

"Oh, look." Jason chuckles, obviously changing the subject. We all watch as Victor attempts to knock the camera down with a broomstick. "He thinks that's going to work? That they won't be recorded?" Jason snickers. "Go ahead, asshole. There are three other cameras in that stairwell and they're all twenty feet up," mutters Jason. "Good fucking luck."

CHAPTER THIRTY-ONE

Ian

WITH THE STING IN MOTION, we watch from our tiny office. Honestly, I'm surprised to see how all three of the Smileys have done exactly what I'd hoped they'd do. On one monitor, we watch as Camille rushes out of her cubicle with her purse and a small box in her hands. My guess is she was already packed up, prepared to flee if need be. I don't think she has any intention of returning to H&S, today or ever. But her plans have been dashed thanks to the plainclothes officers who stop her as she's exiting the building. That was the deal we made with Mills. If at all possible, we'd get them outside the building, in the hopes there'd be less press.

After Victor Smiley gave up on batting down the cameras, we watched him drop the broom and make a break for it, running down the back stairs while Miriam screamed obscenities at him. I called down to inform the police that he'd be exiting out the back. I'm sure they got him too, but I'll make sure of it in a couple minutes.

Finally, we observe Miriam doing her best to calm herself. Straightening her blouse that has risen up in the attempted camera removal process, she steps back onto the thirteenth floor. Switching monitors, we see her about to enter her office, but she changes her mind. Instead, she moves up to Drake's door. It's closed, and for good reason. Brad Mills is in there with a few of Arizona's finest. Unfortunately for Miriam, she doesn't know that. Without knocking, Miriam steps through the door and freezes. I can tell the exact moment she realizes that the jig is up, because she twirls around on one foot and tries to make a run for it. This time it's a uniformed officer who reaches out, grabs her forearm, brings it behind her back, and cuffs her.

"Wow, that was freaking amazing," says Agatha in awe. "I can't believe how well everything worked."

"So far, yeah. Now we just gotta hope Victor did what Miriam told him to do."

"Move the money?"

"If he did, we'll have a record of everything, even account numbers."

"I hope," whispers Agatha.

I reach out and place my hand on the back of her neck and squeeze lightly. "If we don't get it that way, one of those three will give it up. They seem like people who'd throw each other under the bus for less."

"That's very true." Agatha's voice has a sadness to it.

Leaning down, I whisper in her ear, "I'm sorry about your friend, honey."

"Me too, Ian. Me too."

"People suck," grumbles Jason.

It's an unexpected comment that makes us all laugh. Something we all need after such a stressful week and intense morning.

thing we all need after such a stressful week and intense morning.

CHAPTER THIRTY-TWO

AGATHA

FIVE DAYS after Operation Shoe Sting. (*Get it? Shoe sting, not shoe string. Ha!*)

"AND THAT'S how we did it." Sitting at the end of our long table at Murphy's, I hold up my glass of amber goodness and wait for the table full of family to clink glasses in celebration of the fact that the bad guys are behind bars and I'm no longer suspected of stealing a million bucks from my employer.

It's been five days since we were able to unravel and prove me innocent of any and all embezzlement claims made by Drake and Miriam. After the three were arrested, Ian's theory about them throwing each other under the bus was proven correct. They all sang like birds. Thanks to Victor, they were able to locate the money. Miriam was fingered as the ringleader by both Victor and Camille, I mean, Kate. Miriam, surprisingly, kept her mouth shut. She was, apparently, more loyal than the other two.

"So, what happens next?" asks Violet. "Are you going back to work for H&S?"

"No way," grumbles Ian.

He's still angry about the way they treated me. Probably angrier than I am, to be honest. It turns out Miriam has been sabotaging me for years, telling Drake lies about me, my work ethic, and my intelligence, all to keep me right where I was, close to Camille's cubicle. Drake claimed to be as much a victim as I was, but Brad Mills didn't buy it. He fired Drake after he saw the footage of Drake's profanity-laden responses during Ian's performance in conference room three.

Mr. Mills also approached me about returning to work, "with a promotion, of course." I'm sure he realizes that I could sue. I was wrongfully terminated and I was skipped over for promotions numerous times, all because Drake was too busy sleeping in his office and having affairs to take the time to get to know his employees. In the end, I told Brad Mills I didn't feel like working at H&S was in my best interest and that I hoped he would clear my employment record of anything disparaging that Miriam and Drake cooked up about me. I also told him that I expected a glowing recommendation for any future job opportunities. The truth is, though, I *should* sue. Ian wants me to. My sisters and father want me to, but it seems like it'll just bring back all of the emotional stuff and will prolong all of this. I just want to move forward from here.

"No, I'm not going back to work for H&S." I turn to Ian and smile. "I'm going to become a private dick."

I turn to my family and watch the varied reactions to my declaration. Keely spits out the drink she was in the middle of taking. "Private dick?" She giggles.

Lainie looks surprised, Sadie throws her head back, laughing, Violet winks at me, and my dad just smiles and says, "You'd be a natural, sweetie."

I smile back.

"Your mom always said you were going to be a cop."

"Jesus. Please, no. *Not* a cop," groans Keely. She's got a thing against cops.

Ignoring my baby sis, I ask, surprised, "She did?"

"Yep, either that or a spy." He chuckles.

"Well, she tried the spy game a few weeks ago. Disguise and all," Ian says as he wraps his arm around my shoulders.

"Oh, I can't wait to hear about this." Keely scoots up closer to the table, leaning in to listen. "Spill, sis."

"Okay, well..." So I tell them about my feeble attempt to sneak back in to H&S to gather evidence disguised as a caterer. I also tell them about the stakeout and the six hours Ian and I spent sitting outside of the Smileys' place in Mountainaire, Arizona. I didn't mention the hanky-panky in the back seat at about hour three.

What? We had to do something to stay awake.

"So, Ian?" Lainie asks as she holds my free hand. "What's next for you? Are you going back to Phoenix?"

Here we go. Leave it to Lainie to cut right to the chase. Hell, Ian and I haven't even discussed what's going to happen next.

I slowly turn my head to see his arched brow directed at me. Holding my hand over my heart, I say, pleadingly, "I didn't put her up to that. She's a free spirit."

"Damn straight," grumbles Keeton.

God, I love that she found her person. Someone who loves her with his whole heart. I know he'd take a bullet for her. Literally. I've never, ever, seen her happier than she is right now, and no one is more deserving than she is. The truth is, I feel that way about my entire family. We all deserve love—to find our person. The question is, did I find mine?

"Well, honestly, I don't know," Ian says to Lainie.

My face falls a little bit, but I do my best to hide the disappointment. He's trying to let me down easy. Now I wish Lainie had kept her free-spirited trap shut.

He continues, "I think it's something that Agatha and I should discuss privately, but what I will say is it's really her decision. I want to be with her, however she'll have me."

"Aww," coos every female at the table, and possibly my dad.

"Really?" I feel my stupid eyes burn with tears. *There's no crying at Murphy's.*

"Really," he says, leaning close. "I love you, Agatha Palmer."

"Y-you do?" I squeak. That's it, the tears are a-coming. I can't hold 'em back. Sniffling, I whisper in his ear, "Me too, Ian. Me too."

Ian pulls back suddenly, holding up his glass. "Well, I'm happy to report I'll be putting my place on the market and moving north. How's that?" he asks, looking right at Lainie.

"Good. That's great." Lainie clinks her glass against Ian's. "Welcome to the family, big brother."

"Oh, shit," I mumble.

"Shit just got real, eh, sis?" Keely says as she leans halfway across the long table to tap Ian's glass.

Absolutely. Yes. Shit just got real.

CHAPTER THIRTY-THREE

Ian

ONE MONTH later

TRUE TO MY WORD, I put my place on the market and it sold in just three days. A small part of me wished I'd had a little more time, but that'd be the scared pussy part of me. Selling my house and moving in with a woman I've known for only a couple of months is a risk, but the more time I spend with Agatha, the more I like her. And I mean that. I *like* her. A lot. Yes, I love her too, but to like someone *and* love them, that's saying something.

Honest to God, I can't believe my luck. Who'd have thought that one consulting job could change my life so drastically? Not me. I assumed I'd spend the rest of my life alone, just hooking up with random women, never feeling anything more than lust.

I get everything with Agatha: lust, love, passion, and sass. I get sexy Agatha, irritated Agatha, inquisitive Agatha, and fiercely loyal Agatha. I think I love that part of her most of all. I sincerely think she'd take a bullet for me, and she absolutely knows I'd take one for her. Something Catherine didn't seem to understand—about me, anyway.

In retrospect, I'm not sure I actually liked Catherine. She was always so negative. Agatha is the opposite. Agatha's fun to be with; she's always up for an adventure, whether it's a hike around Lake Powell or rummaging through a dusty antique shop looking for a treasure or making love in the middle of the day. I've loved those times together but my favorite moments with her are when we're just out of bed and we're sitting on her porch drinking coffee, doing the crossword together. I've never felt more intimate with a woman than at that moment. Plus, damn she's smart. Agatha's a crossword wizard. I feel like a genius if I'm able to come up with one correct crossword response.

She's not just fun, though. She's passionate about the people in her life. Agatha loves with her whole heart. She can't disguise love because it radiates off her. It's been a long time since I've been surrounded by family like this. As an only child to a couple who had me in their early forties and who thought they'd never have a child, I was showered with love and affection. I was spoiled, for sure. Sadly, my time with them was too short. I lost my mom when I was eighteen and my dad two years later. So, yeah, I've been on my own a long time, Catherine notwithstanding.

Agatha has given me back that sense of family and unconditional love. Not only that, she cooks for me. Sure, that sounds kind of sexist, but that's not how I look at it. Growing up, my mom was always cooking and baking sweet things for me and my dad. It's how she showed love and probably why the sweet tooth is so strong in this one. So, when Agatha surprises me with a plate of oatmeal chocolate chip cookies, or with a roast, pota- toes, and carrots, my heart swells. One night she made her own homemade lasagna, her mom's recipe, and I wanted to drive her to Vegas right then and marry her. So, yeah, food = love, for me, at least. It's why I make her breakfast every morning, and by make, I mean I drive to Sadie Cakes Bakery or to the store to get things she likes.

Besides our domestic changes (i.e. bliss) post embezzle-gate, our careers have had to shift as well. My employer certainly wasn't happy about the change, but I assured them that I could hop on a plane from wherever I lived. My boss at Phoenix was impressed with Agatha's work too. So much so, she offered her a job working right alongside me and Jason on jobs dealing with embezzlement. Agatha was a real asset when it came to following the money trail. When I told her she had a job if she wanted, I don't think I've ever seen anyone so excited. "OMG!" she squealed. "I'm going to be a real-life private dick!" She jumped up and down, clapping her hands furiously. By the time she ran to me and threw herself in my arms, I was almost as excited as she was. "We should totally start our own detective agency. We could call it Burke-Palmer Investigations." She said *Investigations* in breathless anticipation. It was hot as fuck.

In the meantime, she's been doing the books for Beth at Class Act Catering at a very discounted price. When I asked Agatha why she'd do the work for so little, she said, "Because Beth gave me a job even after hearing I was accused of stealing money. She told me 'her gut believed me' and that was that. I'd do it for free, but Beth insists I charge her something." Who can fault any of that? I sure can't.

Not only that, at the encouragement of her sister, Lainie,

Agatha has also taken up writing. She's currently knee-deep in a mystery novel about a murderous embezzler. I'd find it funny except I've already read her first three chapters, and I have to admit, I'm intrigued.

The good thing is, she's got some time now thanks to the settlement from H&S, specifically Brad Mills. Mills didn't even bother with attorneys. A little over a week after Miriam, Camille, and Victor were arrested, a courier showed up at Agatha's door with legal documents and an offer to settle. She was just going to sign the damn papers without reading them as soon as she saw the six-figure sum, just north of two hundred and fifty thousand dollars. I intervened, urging her to read the small print. She read it, and so did I. Neither of us found anything out of the ordinary in the contract. No surprise, there was nondisclosure wording stating she would not be able to speak with the press or write a tell-all about the "incident." There's no chance Agatha would do either of those things, and since the press had already gotten wind of the embezzlement story, it's even less likely. I theorize Drake was the one who spilled the beans. Three days after signing, a large check arrived by the same courier and her writing career began.

Now she doesn't have to worry about money, at least for the time being. But her financial security doesn't mean we shouldn't share expenses. Am I right? Especially if those expenses increase. That is, if I can talk her into buying a bigger place. While I love the cozy aspect of her tiny bungalow, the place makes me feel like a giant living in a hobbit's house. The good news? I've nearly got her talked into doing it. *Nearly* is the operative word. One minute she thinks it's fun to look at new house listings on the internet, the next minute, she doesn't. Honestly, I think she's holding back because she's afraid to make such a big move without a definite commitment from me. I get that. I do. I guess I already feel committed. It's why I drove down to

Phoenix like a bat out of hell to put up a For Sale sign on my place. I was ready.

I am ready. I also think it means I'm going to have to make a decision. And a move. I need to make a grand gesture so she knows I'm in this for the long haul, and I've got just the thing.

Ian

"IAN? What are we doing up here at this time of night?"

"Having a picnic."

"A picnic? At midnight? At Lake Powell?"

"Sure, why not? The weather is perfect, and it's Saturday night. Neither of us has to get up early in the morning. I thought it'd be romantic." I set the picnic basket down and pause. With my hands on my waist, I ask her, "Wait. Are you saying you don't like romance?"

"Of course, I love romance, especially when it's you, Ian. It's just—it's sort of cold up here. May in northern Arizona is nice during the day. At night?"

"Here." I pull off my thick cardigan sweater and hold it open for her to slide inside. I knew she'd need it. She's right about the cold nights.

"Thanks." She eagerly slips the sweater on, pulling it close to her body. Once it's wrapped around her, she shoves her hands into the side pockets. Suddenly, she freezes and stares at me.

"What's wrong?" I already know, but I want to see what she says, does.

Slowly, one of Agatha's hands moves out of the pocket. She seems to be clutching something. I wonder what it could be? Turning her hand until her palm is up, she slowly uncurls her fingers. It's then that I see it. Something shiny in her open palm. "What's this?" she says in a raspy voice.

"Hmm." I tap my chin. "Let me take a look." I remove the ring from her palm and kneel in front of her. I look up and see that her hands are over her mouth. Her eyes are huge and watering. God, I hope that's a good sign.

"Honey?"

A sob escapes her, but she says nothing.

"'Nothing behind me, everything ahead of me.' Jack Kerouac ended that quote by saying 'as is ever so on the road.' If I could rewrite the ending for us, I'd say, Nothing behind me, everything ahead of me, as is ever with my Agatha. I've never felt so lucky, so happy, Agatha. I thought my chance at finding love, true and lasting love, had long since passed, but the minute you looked at me on the street that day, I had hope." I reach out and take her left hand in mine. "Make me the happiest man in the entire world and marry me, honey. Please?"

I watch her swallow, her throat bobbing up and down as she does. She squeezes her eyes shut, and a tear slides down her cheek. I'm holding my damn breath. Is she going to say no?

"That was, hands down, the most romantic proposal I've ever heard. The fact that it was for me, directed at me, makes me want to pinch myself. I wish you'd recorded it."

"We did!" yells a familiar female voice from somewhere beyond the tree line.

Agatha's smile turns into a smirk, then back to a smile. "You invited my family? To our proposal?"

"I did, but they aren't allowed to come out from hiding until you've said yes. So, the ball's in your court. Do you want to drink the champagne I brought, or do you want to punish them for loving you almost as much as I do?"

"Oh, Ian." Agatha wraps her arms around me, whispering in my ear. "Let's make 'em wait. Yes, I'll marry you, you sexy old man."

"I'm not old. I can keep up with *you*." I reach back behind her to pinch her bottom.

"Ouch," she giggles. "You can more than keep up with me. Thank you for this. It's perfect. The fact that you included my family in this tells me everything I need to know. Only *my* person would do that for me."

"Your person," I say, knowing what she means. I've read the letter from her mom. I know what that expression means to her.

"You're my person too, Agatha."

We kiss under the moon overlooking Lake Powell.

"Good. Now, let's put them out of their misery. Pop the cork, fiancé."

"I like the sound of that." Standing up, I yell, "She said yes!"

"Thank fuck," mutters one of her sisters. Keely, if I had to guess. She's got a mouth like a sailor.

Once her father, four sisters, Keeton, and Sadie's pompous boyfriend, Andrew, all stand around us, we toast and drink champagne as we look down over the lake that is perfectly illuminated by the moon. I don't ever remember a time when I've been happier. While I don't know the Palmers all that well yet, I know they're happy for us too. There's also an underlying sense of sadness, like someone is missing. I know what it is. While everyone else is talking and drinking, I pull Agatha a few feet away, so I can say, "I love you, honey."

"I love you too, Ian."

"Is it okay that we're up here? That I proposed up here?" I look out over the lake.

"Oh." She looks up into my eyes. I can see her gray eyes shimmer. "Ian. It's perfect. I feel especially close to her up here, so it's like she's with us right now."

I nod, then lean down to kiss her lips. "That's one reason why I chose this place."

"What's the other reason?"

I swear she can read my mind.

"The first time we came up here... that's the moment I knew I loved you."

I hear her sniffle, so I wrap my arms around her and hold her close.

"Me too, Ian. Me too."

~

"MOM WOULD HAVE TOTALLY LOVED YOU." Agatha says on the ride home.

"Yeah?"

"Oh, yeah. And it's not because you're hot, or because of the romantic proposal at Lake Powell, or because your favorite book is *On the Road*, or that you kept me out of prison." She laughs. "It's because she trusted me, well, all of us, to find the kind of love that she and Dad had—the real kind."

I turn to gaze at my girl. "You think I'm hot?"

Agatha's hand moves to her mouth as an uncontrollable giggle escapes. "That's what you got from that? You want to know if I think you're hot?"

I shrug. "Sure. Why not? I'm old. I need all the encouragement I can get."

She releases an adorable cackle. "You're not old, honey. You can keep up with me."

"I more than keep up with you. How do you feel about having sex on your front porch? Do you think your wicker can take it?"

I listen to her laugh all the way home. It's the loveliest, most joyous sound I've ever heard, and knowing I'll get to hear it for the rest of my life... How did I get so lucky?

CHAPTER THIRTY-FIVE

AGATHA

I'M ENGAGED!

Not only that, I'm engaged to the absolute perfect man for me. And his proposal? Also perfect. Yes, I know I keep saying that word, but if the shoe fits....

I can't believe he proposed and, not only that, he proposed at Lake Powell. My heart is so full right now. He even invited my family. How did I get so lucky? I never thought I'd meet a man like Ian Burke, ever. Not only is the man hot and sexy, that's not even the best part of him. No, the best part, or should I say parts, are his heart and his head. His heart because it's filled with love for me, and his head because a) brains are sexy and b) because he thinks of everyone else before he thinks of himself.

I look down at the ring and sigh. It's beautiful and rather delicate.

"Do you like the ring?" he asks tentatively.

"I do. It looks old." Ian's driving us home from Lake Powell.

His face is serious. I think I may have said the wrong thing. "I don't mean it looks *old*. I mean it has an antique look about it."

"It is old. It was my mom's and her mother's before that."

"Oh, Ian," I squeak, trying my best to keep my emotions in check. But, why should I? The man just gave me his mom's ring. "Th-thank you." I'm sniffling now, doing my best to keep the tsunami of tears that are threatening at bay.

I feel his warm hand over mine, so I turn my hand, palm up, until our fingers are intertwined. "I'm glad you like it."

Wait one dang second. "You didn't give this ring to Catherine?"

He looks over at me again with an expression that says everything I need to know. "One," he pulls my hand up toward his face and kisses it, "I'd never give you *Catherine's* ring. Two, I never had the inclination to give Catherine this ring. It never occurred to me."

"It didn't? Why not?"

Ian chuckles. "I'm starting to wonder if you're trying to tell me something. We can go pick out a different ring, honey. I just thought—"

"No." I squeak again, but I recover because I don't like where this conversation is going. "You *know* how much family means to me, Ian Burke. You had to know what giving me *this* ring would mean to me."

"Yes. I thought it would mean a great deal to you—as much as it means to me."

"Okay." I release a sigh. "Then don't ever, ever, ever, think I want another ring. I love this one so much, and not only because it's a family ring. I love it because *you* gave it to me. My question was just about you and Catherine. Why didn't you give this to her?"

"My sweet girl...." He pauses. "To be completely honest, I

don't know why I didn't give her the ring. I meant what I said, it never occurred to me. Maybe I knew."

"Knew what?"

"She would never have appreciated the gesture. Besides, she wasn't my person."

I gasp. "Really?"

"Really. It would have felt wrong giving this to her," he says, looking down at our joined hands. "I'm not sure I ever felt like Catherine and I were going to ride off into the sunset together. But, you, my sweet Agatha." He kisses my hand again. "You're it for me."

Oh, holy shit. My chin is quivering, and I'm not going to be able to keep my voice even, but I try when I say, "Ian, you're it for me too."

"So, you like the ring?" he asks again, and that makes me laugh.

"I love the damn ring, Ian. Geesh." And I do. It's a simple solitaire diamond set in either white gold or platinum. I'll ask him about that another time. The diamond is impressive. Oh, hell, I'll ask. "How many carats are we talkin' here, stud?" I might as well try to make light of it.

"I don't know a lot about the ring, but I read the certificate when I got it from my safety deposit box. The main stone is about one carat, and with the smaller diamonds on either side of it it's over that, obviously. It's got a platinum band in an Art Deco design. It was made in 1921. I'll let you read more about it. There's also a letter from my mom to my future bride."

"Really? That's so sweet."

Ian gives me a gentle smile. "She was sweet. You'd have liked her. She..."

I wait for him to finish.

"She was a wonderful mom, just like you're going to be."

I gasp. Twice in one car ride. It's got to be a record. "We've never talked about kids, have we?"

"Nope. Not yet."

"You want them? Kids?"

"Do you?" he asks tentatively.

"I do. Of course I do. How many?"

Ian chuckles. "Are we deciding that now?"

"We might as well. You're not getting any younger."

I watch as Ian throws his head back and a rumbling, sexy laugh emerges. "True. How 'bout six?"

"Kids? Six kids? Are you crazy?"

"I was always taught to start high."

"You *are* high if you think I'd push out six children." I giggle at my own statement. "How about one kid?"

"Four."

"Two."

"Three."

"Three."

"Really?" He's smiling from ear to ear. "Three?"

"I'm open to three, but let's start with one and see how that goes. I think parenting is harder than it looks."

"Agreed. Let's start working on that tonight."

"I'm on the pill. It'll take a while for that to get out of my system. Do you really want to start right away? Before we're married?"

"Yes, honey. I want to start everything with you as soon as you're ready."

Oh, my God. He's so sweet.

"But first, we need to look for a larger house. One that'll hold us, three kids, and a couple of dogs."

"Dogs?"

"I had a dog when I was a kid, and I've always wanted another one."

"Well, you've got it all figured out, now haven't you?"

Pulling into our driveway, Ian shuts off the car and turns to face me. "I didn't. Not until I met you, Agatha. Before you, I thought I'd live alone, never realizing what was possible, but you've shown me what happiness looks like. I want to jump in headfirst with you, Aggie."

"Okay," I whisper. "Okay, Ian. Headfirst."

I'VE BEEN ENGAGED for two weeks, and I've never been happier. Ian is here with me full-time now, since his place sold so quickly. I'm not sure that'll be the case with mine. We listed it five days ago and we've only had one showing so far. I guess not a lot of people want a tiny bungalow with one bathroom and barely two bedrooms, but we'll see.

In the meantime, Ian is ready to buy. He wants to use the money from the sale of his place for a down payment on our new place, so we've been house hunting since the day after the engagement. It's all happening so quickly. We found a place just outside of town that we both love. The owners are ready to part with the four bedroom, four bath home for a great price. Ironically, it was Miriam's rental property out on Reflection Canyon.

Speaking of Miriam and her gang of hoodlums, they've all been arraigned and, from what Ian said, are all out on bail. Each of them has to wear an ankle monitoring device while they await trial. I know that firsthand because I ran into Camille one day when I was shopping in Flagstaff. She was wearing shorts and flip-flops, so you couldn't miss the clunky device. My immediate response was to wave and run over to her, but then I remembered we weren't best friends anymore, so I stayed put.

When she stepped closer, she scowled at me. At *me*.

Choosing to be a bigger person, I said, "Hello, Cam—I mean, Kate."

"Agatha," she sneered. "Perfect, princess Agatha. Everybody loves Agatha. Until they thought you were a thief. Ha! That was awesome."

Perfect, princess Agatha? What the hell? She's mental. "Why me? I certainly didn't deserve to be framed." I might as well ask her that. It's been the one thing I just couldn't wrap my head around.

"Jesus, you're so full of yourself. Poor Agatha with her dead mom and stupid crush on Trent," she says mockingly. "I guess I can tell you. You were gullible and convenient."

Okaaaaay.

I haven't spoken to Trent at all since I was fired. Not even after I was cleared. He's reached out to me via text message, but I haven't responded. What is there to say?

"I've got a little secret about your precious Trent," she whisper-hisses.

I wait. No reason to say anything.

"I was fucking Trent the entire time I worked there."

"Oh." That does surprise me.

She leans in closer, but I stand my ground.

"One time, we did it in your office. On your desk."

Okaaaaay. "Gross," I mutter.

"It was a little gross," she snickers. "The guy sucks in bed. I probably saved you. I shouldn't have."

I stare at my former work colleague. I no longer see a friend or any reason to listen to any more from her. "Well, good luck to you, Kate."

"Fuck you," she mutters.

Well, maybe I've got one more thing to say. "No. Fuck you. I thought of you as my dearest friend. I would have done anything for you. You chose to steal and to frame me." I turn to leave. "Goodbye, Kate. Enjoy prison."

"Fuck you."

I guess there's nothing more to say. I left the items I planned to buy that day on a random shelf and walked out the door. With my head held high, I speed-walked to my car, hopped in, and drove off into the sunset. No. Seriously. It was the actual sunset.

The truth is, I'm lucky. I get to drive home to a man who loves me and who wouldn't be in my life if it weren't for Camille and her diabolical parents, so for that, I should thank her, but I don't think I will, especially now. Nope. I don't think she'd understand the significance.

The minute I get home, I yell for him. "Ian?"

"Bedroom," he shouts back.

I step into my room, to a view that's beyond anything I've ever seen. It's Ian Burke lying on top of my quilt in only a pair of athletic shorts. Nothing else. He's wearing his dark-rimmed glasses, his hair is a bit messy in a very sexy way, and he's got a book on his chest. And not just any book. He's reading *Pride and Prejudice.*

Be still my heart.

"Whatcha doing, honey?" I say a little shyly. I'm not sure why. Maybe because the sight of him took my breath away.

"Reading. Waiting."

"Waiting? For what?"

"You."

"For me? For how long?"

"My entire life."

Well, now, what else does a girl need to hear? Absolutely nothing. "Me too."

The Importance of Being Ernie with Bonus Book The Importance of
Being Kennedy's

Quirky Girl

<u>For a complete list of Kayt's books, visit:</u>

<u>Kayt's Website</u>

ACKNOWLEDGMENTS

Thank you to Olivia at Hot Tree Editing for editing this book from start to finish.

And an extra special thank you to Becky at Hot Tree Promotions for your advice, expertise, and your positivity.

And for my beta readers. Thank you so much for your time and feedback!

ABOUT THE AUTHOR

How did it all start? Well, I love reading and one day I was searching for a book. A book about a certain type of woman and a specific kind of man and I couldn't find it so, I wrote it. I called it Game Changer and it couldn't have been a more appropriate title. It changed my life in many ways. While my real job is teaching young people, my fun job is conjuring up characters and situations to write about.

My goal, as a writer, is to write stories that relate to all of us, to make readers laugh and maybe cry sometimes. I hope my readers can escape into a fantasy, one that's actually possible. Sure, some of the stories could be dubbed "Insta-love" stories but that's okay. I fell in love with my husband pretty damn fast and with my daughter the second I saw her. So, it's a thing, I swear.

Please Follow Me on these social media sites. Following on BookBub to learn about special book deals.

I love hearing from you!

Thank you so much for reading Agatha and Ian's story! When I start a story, it begins with an outline, notes, and lots of crazy thoughts running through my head. When I actually start writing, the characters take over, leading me through the story like they're holding my hand—guiding me. The process is exciting and cathartic. With that said, I hope you enjoy the story.

If you did, please go to my website, www.kaytmiller.com, and join my newsletter so you can be the first to know what's coming up next. And...

Please, leave a review!

No matter how you feel about the book, please leave a review. Reviews are important to authors and other readers. I, for one, read them and sure, it takes me a week or two to get over the bad ones, but it's how we learn, right? Seriously, I've gained great insight in this process through your eyes. So, post on Amazon or Goodreads. You can also contact me via my Website, or in an email if you've really got to vent. ;)

Prologue

Squatting down behind one of my three display cases, I arrange a new flavor of cupcake front and center. "Mm, yum," I say, inhaling the delicious scent of caramel and pretzel.

"Sadie, are you sure about that one?" asks my trusty sidekick and co-worker Polly. "It sounds a little gross. And aren't those pretzels going to get mushy sitting on top of all that frosting?"

I know, I know. It doesn't sound like it would taste good but trust me, it does. It's the combination of the salty pretzel and the sweet caramel that make the flavors burst in your mouth. "I'm sure. And I brushed a layer of melted sugar on the bottom of the pretzels to prevent the dreaded mushiness." Then I chuckle because Polly's face tells me everything I need to know. The woman can't hide her feelings no matter how hard she tries. She's a finicky eater. I practically have to beg her to try some of my more, how shall I say—creative—cupcake recipes. She's strictly a vanilla kind of girl. That's okay. Vanilla is probably my biggest seller, so I can't slight it. "They're only for garnish anyway but still tasty with the sugar."

"I know I should trust you. You've got a knack for—"

When the bell over the door chimes, I say, "Can you handle that while I go back for another tray?"

Polly doesn't respond to me but whispers just loud enough for me to hear, "Oh *my*. Hubba-hubba." Polly's voice sounds husky and for my ears only, apparently.

When a deep voice sounds, "Hello," I look up at Polly. As soon as I hear a male voice in the room, I peek up at my friend. She's boy-crazy. Or I guess I should say man-crazy, so when she sees one, she likes, she gets excited. 'Hubba-hubba' is a commonly heard phrase when there's a handsome man in the area.

The woman has no shame when it comes to meeting men. And men make no apologies about the fact their feelings are mutual. I suppose it could be because she's built like a 1950s bombshell with curves and gorgeous platinum blonde hair (because *she's worth it*). That's probably it. When she reaches down to grasp my shoulder, I look up. I want to laugh at my friend's expression because I've seen it before. She's man-crazy. I'd go so far as to say she's a horn-dog. She stares down at me with eyes as big and round as saucers. Then she mouths, *Oh. My. God.* She's met her one true love, *of the week.*

History tells me that I'm going to need to take over from here since she'll be drooling all over the cupcakes if I don't. Wiping my hands on my blue-and-white-striped Sadie Cakes Bakery apron, I stand from my squatted position. "Welcome to Sadie Cakes, how can I..." I stop speaking the moment I see him.

Shit.

No looking back.

Shit.

Shit.

Fuck!

"What are you doing here?"

Ignoring my question, he says, "Rachel. You're a hard woman to find."

Nerves flood my body. *That voice.* I'm instantly queasy. Placing my hand over my stomach, I concentrate on my breathing. *Get yourself under control, Sadie.* But I can't help it. There are times I think if I didn't have bad luck, I'd have no freaking luck at all. Doing my best to appear calm and cool, I say, "I didn't realize I was lost."

His chuckle is deep and rich. The memory of the same deep, rich voice whispering in my ear causes my body to vibrate. My hands are shaking. Not from fear. No. I'm not afraid of this man. Well, let me rephrase that. I'm not afraid he'll physically harm me. No, I'm afraid of my reaction to him. In that way, he's dangerous. *So* damn dangerous.

"It's taken me almost two months to find you. If I'd just read this," he holds up some crumpled, white cloth in his hands, "I'd have found you weeks ago."

I watch as he unfurls the cloth. It's a t-shirt. One of *my* t-shirts that reads *Sadie Cakes Bakery*.

"Where did you...?"

"You left it on the floor of your cabin."

"Oh."

Shit.

Taking in a deep breath, *Courage, Sadie,* I step around the counter and approach him, holding out my hand. "Thank you for returning it."

He pulls it up above his head and out of my reach, which isn't hard for him to do since he's at least ten inches taller than me. Leaning toward me, he says, "You think I came all this way to give you back your shirt?"

"Yes." *No.* But I'm not about to do anything that will draw out this conversation.

"Think again, beautiful."